Praise for

The Fairy-Tale MATCHMAKER

BOOKS BY E. D. BAKER

The *Fairy* → *Tale* MATCHMAKER

THE TRUEST HEART

E.D. BAKER

BLOOMSBURY

NEW YORK LONDON OXFORD NEW DELHI SYDNEY

First published in the United States of America in October 2016
by Bloomsbury Children's Books
Paperback edition published in October 2017
www.bloomsbury.com

Bloomsbury is a registered trademark of Bloomsbury Publishing Plc

For information about permission to reproduce selections from this book, write to
Permissions, Bloomsbury Children's Books, 1385 Broadway, New York, New York 10018
Bloomsbury books may be purchased for business or promotional use. For information on
bulk purchases please contact Macmillan Corporate and Premium Sales Department at
specialmarkets@macmillan.com

The Library of Congress has cataloged the hardcover edition as follows:
Names: Baker, E. D., author.
Title: The truest heart / by E. D. Baker.
Description: New York : Bloomsbury, 2016. | Series: The fairy-tale matchmaker
Summary: Cory Feathering has abandoned the Tooth Fairy Guild she was born
into in favor of choosing her own path as a matchmaker, and now decides to
fight for what she believes in by helping Mary Lambkin find true love.
Identifiers: LCCN 2015040009
ISBN 978-1-61963-849-5 (hardcover) • ISBN 978-1-61963-850-1 (e-book)
Subjects: | CYAC: Tooth Fairy—Fiction. | Fairies—Fiction. | Characters in
literature—Fiction. | Dating services—Fiction. | Humorous stories. |
BISAC: JUVENILE FICTION/Fantasy & Magic. | JUVENILE FICTION/Love &
Romance. | JUVENILE FICTION/Fairy Tales & Folklore/General.
Classification: LCC PZ7.B17005 Tr 2016 | DDC [Fic]—dc23
LC record available at https://lccn.loc.gov/2015040009

ISBN 978-1-68119-574-2 (paperback)

Book design by Ellice Lee and John Candell
Typeset by Newgen Knowledge Works (P) Ltd., Chennai, India
Printed and bound in the U.S.A. by Berryville Graphics Inc., Berryville, Virginia
2 4 6 8 10 9 7 5 3

All papers used by Bloomsbury Publishing, Inc., are natural, recyclable products
made from wood grown in well-managed forests. The manufacturing processes
conform to the environmental regulations of the country of origin.

This book is dedicated to Kim, who inspired this series; to my fans, who ask for more; to Victoria, who is still teaching me so much; and to Brett, who makes me look at things in a different way.

The Fairy Tale MATCHMAKER

THE TRUEST HEART

CHAPTER
1

"Wake up, lazybones," Weegie the woodchuck said, nudging Cory's hand with her cold, wet nose.

Cory woke, startled, expecting to see yet another monster lurking in her bedroom. Instead, she saw the two woodchucks staring at her from the floor by the side of her bed. Although Noodles couldn't talk, a witch's spell had given his girlfriend the ability.

"Hurry up," said Weegie. "I need to go out, unless you want a puddle on your floor."

"I'm coming," Cory said, still half asleep.

Crawling out of bed, she pulled on her robe and started toward the door, yawning. Noodles got there before she did and sat on his haunches, while Weegie paced back and forth beside him. When Cory opened the door to her bedroom, they ran to the front door and turned to look at her accusingly.

The moment she had it open, they ran outside and stopped. "What's wrong?" Cory asked. She stepped onto the porch and gasped when she saw two flower fairies smearing mud across the floor.

Surprised, the fairies stopped to stare.

"Let me at 'em!" cried Weegie. She started to run at the fairies, but the mud was slippery and her feet went out from under her. Skidding across the mud, she collided with a flower fairy dressed all in green. The fairy took off, shrieking. The sound seemed to wake the other fairy, who shook herself and took off after her friend.

"Why am I not surprised?" Cory said, seeing the mess on the porch.

"What is it? What happened?" Blue asked as he staggered to his feet.

Cory's true love had spent the night sleeping on the floor of the main room. The guilds had been harassing Cory and had even tried to kidnap her from the courthouse minutes before she was to testify in front of the big jury. Blue had announced that he was going to arrange for bodyguards to watch over her and had taken the first shift himself.

The guilds had been persecuting Cory for a while now. It had started right after she quit the Tooth Fairy Guild. Mary Mary, the head of the guild, had tried to make her rejoin by threatening her. When that didn't work, she'd punished Cory by taking away her fairy abilities, including her fairy wings. Things only got worse when Cory and her grandfather Lionel got the law involved and pushed until the case went before the big jury.

"Noodles and Weegie caught the flower fairies making a muddy mess on the porch," Cory told Blue as the woodchucks rooted through the mud. "Weegie scared them off."

"Did I hear someone yelling?" Micah said from his bedroom door. Cory's uncle looked as tired as she felt. Three different members of the Itinerant Troublemakers Guild had visited them during the night, which meant that no one had gotten much sleep.

"Just another visit from the Flower Fairy Guild," Cory said as she started to close the door. "I'll clean up the mud after breakfast."

Before Cory had the door fully closed, someone knocked on the other side. Surprised, she pulled it open again. Her grandfather Lionel was standing there, wiping his muddy shoes on the doormat.

"I'm glad to see that you're awake," he said. "Is it too early to come in?"

"No, no, please do," Cory said as she stepped to the side. "We all seem to be up, so we might as well stay up."

"I'll start breakfast as soon as I've gotten dressed," said Micah, closing his bedroom door.

"I'll join you in the kitchen in just a minute," Blue told her, and headed for the bathing room.

Cory led her grandfather to the kitchen. While he took a seat, she started some hot water for tea.

"I saw that you already had a visitor this morning," Lionel said.

"Two visitors, actually," Cory said as she reached for the tea container. "Two flower fairies were muddying up the porch when I let the woodchucks out. But that's nothing compared to last night. Three different members of the Itinerant Troublemakers Guild dropped in. The Thing That Goes Bump in the Night came first. Then it was the Monster Under the Bed. Oh, and then the third one really came to warn me. It was my old friend Harmony Twitchet, who was filling in for the Thing That Scratches at Your Window. She came to tell me that the ITG has sent for its 'Big Baddies' to start plaguing me, as if the ordinary members aren't bad enough."

"Three ITG members in one night!" exclaimed Lionel. "The guilds must really be worried. But that fits in with something I wanted to tell you."

"Here we are!" Micah said as he and Blue walked into the kitchen. "I'm going to make a big pot of cooked oats. Have a seat. Breakfast will be ready in a few minutes."

Cory added tea to the water she'd heated. "Harmony said that the Itinerant Troublemakers Guild has teamed up with the Tooth Fairy Guild and the Flower Fairy Guild, supposedly to stop me from turning people against them."

Lionel nodded. "Our informants have told us that they're inviting the other guilds to 'stand up against guild suppression,' as they call it. The real problem is, they've acquired a great deal of power over the years and are afraid of losing it. Even some of the less forceful guilds are being talked into joining them. The Housecleaning Guild is aligned with them now, as well as the Sandman Guild and that new Belly Button Lint Guild. Very few guilds have actually turned them down. Most just say that they are taking it under consideration. And that brings me to why I stopped by."

Lionel paused to stifle a yawn while everyone waited. "Excuse me. The members of the big jury stayed up all night deliberating. I'm on my way home now, but I wanted to tell you the news before it went public. The case against the guilds is going to trial. Judge Dumpty is about to make the public announcement."

"That was fast," declared Micah. He set a bowl of cooked oats in front of Lionel, then passed out bowls to Cory and Blue.

"When is the trial scheduled to begin?" asked Blue.

"As soon as possible," Lionel told him. "No one believed that the guilds were capable of terrorizing their own members until Cory and Stella Nimble testified. Now the board wants this whole thing settled before the rest of the guilds band together against us."

"I'm going to have to testify again, aren't I?" said Cory.

Lionel nodded. "You'll be one of the first. The prosecuting law upholder will be calling on you any day now."

When someone started pounding on the front door, Blue jumped to his feet. "That should be Macks. He'll be your bodyguard today while I'm at work," he told Cory.

"I'll go meet him," she said, standing up.

"Cory, why don't you stay here and eat your breakfast?" said Micah. "Your cooked oats will get cold. Blue, do you want to ask Macks to join us? If he's going to spend the day here, I think we should all meet him."

Blue nodded and left the room while Cory sat down again. She was sprinkling brown sugar on her cooked oats when her grandfather said, "Who is this Macks person? Have you ever met him before?"

Cory shrugged. "I might have. I've met a number of Blue's friends, but I haven't learned all their names yet."

She looked up as Blue came back into the room. Half ogre and half human, he nearly filled the doorway. Macks followed him into the kitchen and had to stoop to enter. When he turned to face Cory, she remembered seeing him before. He was one of the uglier ogres, with a bulging forehead, a nose like a lumpy potato, ears that stuck out from the sides of his head, and lips so thin on his wide mouth that it didn't look as if he had any at all. Full ogres didn't have to do or say anything to be intimidating.

"Hey," he rumbled when he saw everyone seated at the kitchen table. "What's up?"

"Everyone, this is Macks, a good friend of mine," said Blue. "Cory, you might remember meeting him. He was with the solar-cycle riders when they stopped by the house and ate pie the other day. He was part of your escort to the courthouse yesterday, too."

"Hi, Macks," said Cory.

"Hey, Cory," the ogre said in his deep, scratchy voice. "Got any more of that pie?"

"Sorry," she said with a smile. "It's all gone."

"Macks," said Blue, "this is Cory's grandfather Mr. Feathering and her uncle, Mr. Fleuren."

"Hey," Macks said, nodding at them both.

"Macks is going to stay with you until I come back tonight, Cory," Blue told her. "He can handle anything that comes up, but if something does, I want you to send me a message right away. It would be best if you didn't go out."

"Does this mean that I can't take on any more odd jobs?" said Cory. "My ad is still running in *The Fey Express.*"

Blue shook his head. "No more odd jobs until the trial is over. Helping strangers is definitely out."

After quitting the guild, Cory had taken on odd jobs to earn money. She'd also become a matchmaker at her friend Marjorie's request. Word had spread that she was good at making matches, and she quickly acquired more clients. The day after the Tooth Fairy Guild had taken away her fairy abilities, Cory had learned that she was a Cupid with the ability to find someone's true love. Apparently, being a matchmaker of sorts really was her true calling.

"She can go out tomorrow, though, right?" said Macks. "That party we told you about starts tomorrow morning. Are you going to bring those pies, Cory? You make the best pies."

"Oh, Blue, let's go!" Cory said. "You know I'll be safe with your ogre friends."

"I don't know . . . ," said Blue.

"Ogres don't join guilds," Micah said, looking thoughtful. "And there's little a guild could do to influence one. If they're already your friends, I can't think of anywhere safer."

"If you really want to go, Cory," said Blue, "I'll see about taking the day off so I can take you."

"I'll talk to the board," said Lionel. "You won't have to take the day off if you're assigned to protect her."

Blue was training to be a Fey Law Enforcement Agency officer and could easily be assigned to watch such an important witness. Even so, Cory was grateful. "Thank you, Grandfather," she told him. "It helps having a close relative on the Fey Law Enforcement Agency board."

"Now that that's settled, I have to get to work," said Micah. "I'm giving each student in my first period class five minutes for their oral presentations. We'll need to start as soon as the bell rings if half the class is going to present today. Oh, I almost forgot. Do you have a rehearsal tonight, Cory? Do you need to eat dinner early?"

Cory nodded. "We're working on a new song. I really should be there."

"Then go ahead and eat without me if you need to," said Micah. "I have a faculty meeting after school, so I don't know what time I'll be home."

"Are you going to the party tomorrow, Uncle Micah?" Cory asked him. "You were invited, too, remember?"

Micah shook his head. "Tomorrow is a regular school day," he said. "I can't take off for a party. But I want you to go and have a good time. I really need to head out now. Good-bye, everyone. Stay safe."

"I should go, too," said Lionel. "The putti are probably worried sick about me. If I don't get home soon, they'll be mounting a search party. Putti may be small, but they have big hearts and are the worst worriers you'll ever meet."

"Now that Macks is here, I need to get to work," Blue announced. "If I get there early, I might be able to leave early and I want to get back in time to eat and take you to your rehearsal. No more riding on the pedal-bus until after the trial is over. I don't want to give the guilds even the smallest opportunity to hurt you! If you absolutely have to go somewhere, either your bodyguard or I will take you."

Macks nodded. "I rode my solar cycle. I brought an extra helmet, too, just in case."

Blue gave Cory a quick kiss before starting for the door. "Good-bye, my love. I'll see you tonight."

"'Bye!" said Macks with a wave of his hand.

Blue gave him a funny look and Cory giggled. When the ogre turned to look at her, she told him, "I think he was talking to me."

"Oh!" he said, sounding surprised. "Yeah, that makes sense."

CHAPTER
2

As soon as Blue, Micah, and Lionel were gone, Cory offered Macks a seat. "Would you like a cup of tea or a bowl of cooked oats while I finish my breakfast?"

"Ogres don't drink tea," said Macks. "It gives us indigestion. I'd eat the cooked oats, though."

Cory got another bowl from the cupboard and began to fill it. "Tell me when it's enough," she told the ogre.

He watched intently as she dropped one spoonful after another into the bowl, but didn't say anything until the pot was empty. "That should be enough," he said, although Cory had a feeling he would have taken more if there had been any.

Macks looked surprised when Cory offered him the brown sugar. When he tried a little on the oats, his eyes lit up and he reached for the sugar again. Enough sugar went on the oats to turn them brown, but Macks seemed to love it. "You are a very good cook!" he declared when he'd finished, and proceeded to lick the bowl.

"Thank you," Cory said, remembering that Blue had told her that ogres licked their plates if they thought the food was delicious. She wondered if all of them got indigestion from tea and liked sugar as much as Macks did. It made her think about how little she knew of ogres. Because her own true love was half ogre, Cory thought she really should learn all she could about them.

"Say, I was wondering," Macks said when he handed her the bowl. "Do you usually spread mud on your porch? Some ogres prefer it that way, but I don't remember seeing mud there the other day."

Cory shook her head. "The flower fairies put it there. They've been doing all sorts of things to harass me."

"Do you want me to wash it off?" the ogre asked. "I like working with mud."

"That would be very helpful," Cory told him. "The hose is around back."

"I'll find it," he said.

"And then I'd like to go to the market," said Cory. "If I'm going to make pies to take to the party tomorrow, I need to buy some berries."

"Lots of berries, you mean," said Macks. "You'll need them to make lots of pies!"

While Cory went to her room to get dressed, Macks went to look for the hose. He was still washing off the porch when she came back out, so she washed the dirty dishes and straightened up the kitchen. The ogre was waiting for her when she finished. Grabbing her purse, she followed him outside.

"The porch looks great!" Cory said as she locked the door. "Thank you for cleaning it."

"I enjoyed it," said Macks. "Before we go, there's something I want to set straight."

"What is it?" Cory asked, tucking her keys in her purse.

"I just wanted you to know that I'm not available," the ogre told her. "I have a girlfriend, and you have Blue."

Cory was stunned. "I never thought—"

"I'm telling you this because I know that most girls find me irresistible, and I wouldn't want you to get your hopes up. I had to fend them off with a stick when I was in school. I took that stick everywhere. I named it Ingbar. Blue has been my best friend since we were little gruntlings. My father and his father were best friends, too. I would never do anything to hurt Blue."

Cory shook her head. "I wouldn't, either. I don't know if Blue told you, but we love each other. I'm not interested in anyone but Blue."

"That's a relief!" said Macks. "I thought you might have fallen for me because of my good looks, and the way I washed your porch without being asked."

"Uh, no," Cory said, trying not to laugh.

"You know," Macks said as they stepped off the porch, "most ogres wouldn't let their ogress girlfriends spend time with another ogre. A long time ago male ogres would go on rampages if another male even looked at their girlfriend the wrong way. We don't do that anymore, though. It cost too much to fix everything we broke and our girlfriends would dump us. Now we just get mad and yell a lot."

"Good to know," said Cory.

"If you're ready, I'm going to introduce you to Lucille."

Cory was aghast. "Do you mean that your girlfriend has been waiting out here all this time?"

Macks snorted, knocking the petals off a petunia in the flower bed by the porch. "Lucille isn't my girlfriend! My girlfriend's name is Estel. This is Lucille, my special girl," he said, leading Cory to a solar cycle parked at the curb. "I spent the entire morning polishing her chrome yesterday. You can see your reflection in it. See? Watch out, don't touch anything! I'll scalp the first person who puts fingerprints on her! I don't mean you, of course, but I do want to keep her nice and shiny. She deserves it."

"She is very beautiful," Cory told him. "I feel honored that you're going to let me ride her."

"You should," said Macks. "Very few people get the chance. So tell me, which market do you want to visit?"

"The East Market, I suppose," said Cory. "They have the freshest fruits and vegetables."

"Here, I have an extra helmet you can wear," Macks said, opening a compartment in the back of Lucille. "It's not as nice as mine, but it should fit your little head."

"Thanks," Cory said, biting her lip so she didn't laugh out loud. The helmet that Macks was putting on his own head was the one he had worn the day before. It looked like a troll skull with sharp horns and had paint the color of blood splashed on it to make it look more fearsome. Like Macks's head, the helmet was huge. The helmet he'd handed to her was a lot like Blue's, with a smoother shape and no bumps or protrusions. It *was* neon green, but then she supposed she couldn't have everything.

Riding behind Macks was a lot different from riding with Blue. When Blue was driving, Cory snuggled up to him and rode with her arms around him and her cheek pressed to his back. Macks was a lot bigger and smelled like an ogre. She had no desire to get close to him, or to touch him if she could help it. Even if she'd wanted to, she couldn't have wrapped her arms around him because he was just too big. Instead, she rode holding on to the seat, trying to balance with each turn and not fall off with every bump. Lucille was a nice solar cycle, but Cory much preferred riding with Blue.

Cory had scarcely gotten used to riding with Macks when she spotted a young woman who reminded her of Mary Lambkin, one of her matchmaking clients. A few minutes later, a vision of Mary popped into her head. They were turning a corner when the face of Jasper Wilkins appeared in the vision as well. Cory had seen Mary and Jasper in a vision once before. Then the last time she'd visited the courthouse, she'd seen Jasper walking down the courthouse hallway. Although she didn't know who he was then, she had learned about him by asking around. If she was seeing their faces again, she was supposed to match them up as soon as possible. When she *saw* a vision and didn't make a match, that vision would come more and more frequently until she couldn't think of anything else.

Macks turned a corner and Cory started to slip. Startled, she tightened her grip on the seat. Her heart was pounding when she resolved to pay attention to the ride. Although the East Market wasn't too far from Micah's house, Cory thought the ride seemed to take forever. Part of that was because she was so uncomfortable, and part was because of the attention they were attracting. At first she thought people were staring at the ogre riding in front of her, but when they stopped at an intersection to let three fairies and a gnome cross, she saw that the people on the sidewalk were pointing at her.

It was worse when they got to the market. She was handing the helmet she'd used to Macks when she heard people whispering behind her.

"That's her, I tell you. She's the one that's causing all the trouble."

"Can you believe it? Why would anyone want to destroy the guilds?"

"Those poor fairies! Spreading lies about them like that. She should be ashamed of herself."

Macks must have heard them, too, because he turned around and glared at the whispering people. When Cory saw them, they were running away.

"Let's find those berries and get out of here," said Macks. "I don't like the riffraff."

Cory gave him a grateful look as he held the door open. She didn't know if she could have come here without someone who was so obviously on her side.

Unlike the West Market that was little more than a roof covering an area where vendors could sell their products from their carts, the East Market was made up of two buildings, each with walls and doors and big windows looking out onto the road. Inside it was filled with tables that the vendors rented. Macks had parked his solar cycle next to the building where food was sold. Vendors in the other building sold clothes and jewelry and footwear.

When they stepped into the building, Cory found that they had entered at the opposite end from where fresh produce was displayed. They'd have to walk the entire length of the building to find berries. The vendors closest to them were frost fairies selling frozen food. Cory kept her head down, hoping they wouldn't notice her in the crowd. She and Macks were leaving that section of the market when a frost fairy selling frozen fish and meat spotted her.

"What are you doing here?" she said, looking at Cory with open dislike.

"Just keep going," Macks told Cory.

"I was talking to you!" the frost fairy shouted when Cory and Macks walked away. Cory glanced back just as the frost fairy raised her arm.

"Watch out!" Macks said, stepping between Cory and the frost fairy.

Cory could hear the hiss of frost being cast across the room and the crackle as it started to form on Macks. The ogre growled and lunged toward the table. The frost fairy threw herself on the ground, out of the ogre's reach. When Macks turned back to Cory, the side of his face and neck were white with frost.

"Oh, no! That must really hurt!" Cory cried.

"What?" said Macks, turning his head to look around.

"Your face! She frosted it!" said Cory.

The ogre reached up to touch his cheek. "Huh!" he grunted. "Better me than you. Frost doesn't hurt me. I hear it bites soft skins like you."

Cory was confused until she realized that he meant "frostbite." It was the reason no one wanted to get on the bad side of a frost fairy, and here she had the entire guild aligned against her!

As Macks hustled Cory through the building, past the tables where fairies sold honey and wax candles and elves sold milk and cheese, she wondered if coming to the market had been such a good idea. She'd known the guilds were mad at her, but she didn't know that individual fairies were as well. And the things they were saying weren't at all true. She didn't want to bring down the guilds, just make them treat their members the way everyone should be treated. She certainly hadn't told any lies!

The fresh produce section was crowded when Macks and Cory reached it, so it took a few minutes to find the farmer selling berries. Cory saw Jonas McDonald there, selling his gossiping grapes, but he had so many customers that she didn't think he saw her. Apparently, he had taken her suggestion and was selling them as curiosities.

The man selling berries was only three tables past Jonas, and was nearly as busy. Cory and Macks waited until it was their turn. The man barely glanced at Cory when she finally bought the berries. She was heading toward the exit, beginning to think that she and Macks might be able to leave without any more incidents, when a fairy selling fresh flowers saw her.

"How dare you show your face here!" the fairy shouted, drawing everyone's eyes to Cory. "You have a lot of nerve!"

"Let's get out of here," Macks said as the flower fairy reached under her table.

Macks and Cory were still in range when the flower fairy yanked the flowers out of a bucket and heaved the dirty water at them. Some of the water hit Cory, but most of it splashed Macks. He was dripping when he turned and roared at the fairy, "Now cut that out!"

Suddenly, the way in front of them was clear. Macks growled when they passed a nymph trying to enter the building, making her quake and back away. When Cory and Macks reached Lucille, the ogre shook his head and scowled. "You know, I don't care what they do to me, but now they're making me get dirty water on Lucille! This makes me really mad!" He turned to face the building and raised his voice to a roar. "If I ever see those blasted fairies again, I'll roll them up and use them as beach balls!"

Half the windows on that side of the building shattered when he roared. Of the few people who had come outside to watch Cory and Macks leave, three people fainted and the rest ran away as fast as they could.

"Probably wouldn't work, though," Macks muttered as he took his seat on Lucille. "They wouldn't stay rolled up and I'm sure they'd yell a lot."

"Wouldn't rolling people up be considered a rampage?" asked Cory.

"Oh, no," Macks said, shaking his head. "Rampages are much worse."

Much to Macks's delight, Cory spent the rest of the day baking. She made eleven pies—ten to take to the party and one to eat at home. Macks had already eaten half of the eleventh pie before Blue pulled up on his solar cycle.

"I stopped at my house and got a change of clothes," he said, showing Cory his suitcase. "I even remembered pajamas. Sleeping in the clothes you're going to wear to work is not a good idea. Hey, Macks, how did it go today?"

"Fine," said his friend. "We went to the market and got berries. Cory made pies for tomorrow. I had a piece to make sure they were as good as the last ones." The ogre winked at Cory and smacked his lips. "They were! I'll be heading out now. See you tomorrow at the party!"

"You went to the market?" said Blue as his friend left the house.

Cory nodded. "I needed to get the pies baked early because I'll be at rehearsal tonight. I think next time I'll ask you or Micah to go. I know the guilds are mad at me, but I didn't know that other people are, too."

"What do you mean?" Blue said.

"People I'd never seen before were accusing me of lying and trying to destroy the guilds. A frost fairy was aiming for me, but Macks got between us and she frosted his face. Then a flower fairy threw water from a pail at us. Most of the water hit Macks. He's actually a very nice person," said Cory. "I'm sorry he got Lucille dirty. Are you hungry? I thought I'd heat up some soup and make sandwiches for supper."

"I'd like that, as long as I can have a piece of pie afterward! Is there anything I can do to help?" he said, following her into the kitchen.

Cory smiled and handed him the bread. "You can make the sandwiches if you want."

Blue set the loaf on the table and went in search of a knife. "I'll have you know I'm an expert sandwich maker. Ground nut butter or cheese? Those are my specialties!"

While Cory heated the soup, Blue made a stack of sandwiches. When they finally sat down to eat, Cory asked, "So, were you assigned to watch over me tomorrow?"

Blue grinned. "I was. I can't drink cider when I'm

on duty, but I wasn't planning to drink it anyway. I need my wits about me all the time now. We never know what the guilds are going to do next."

"I can't imagine they'll try anything at an ogre party," said Cory.

"I don't think they will, either," replied Blue. "But you never can tell."

They rode Blue's solar cycle to Olot's cave, where the band always held their rehearsals. Olot was an ogre and was married to a lovely young woman named Chancy, the former lady-in-waiting to a wicked queen. Blue had met them both before, but this was the first time he was going to attend a rehearsal.

"Are you sure they won't mind?" Blue asked as he turned the solar cycle onto the road leading up the side of the mountain.

"Not at all," said Cory. "Skippy's girlfriends come to all the rehearsals and no one has ever complained. Chancy will be there, too, but then it is her home. You already know who everyone is. I think you'll have fun. The cave isn't far from here. Look! That's the path to the cave the three little pigs just bought from Olot. I wonder how Olot and Chancy like their new neighbors."

As soon as Blue had parked his cycle, Cory ran to the door of the cave. Chancy answered her knock and smiled when she saw that Blue was with her.

"We heard about what happened at the courthouse," said Chancy. "So we wondered if you'd be safe coming here. I'm so glad to see that Blue brought you. Come in, Blue! Welcome to our home!"

"Did I hear you say that Johnny Blue is here?" boomed Olot as he tromped down the hallway. "Well, what do you know? A real celebrity coming to our cave."

Blue laughed as he shook Olot's hand. "I think you and the other members of Zephyr are the celebrities. I've heard you play, and I've seen how much your audiences love you."

"No more than your audiences love you," Olot told him. "You have to be the best trumpet player around. Come in and have a seat. I'm sure Cory has told you that we're working on a new song tonight. We have a full lineup of gigs and need something new to keep our audiences coming back."

Cory took Blue's hand and led him into the main room of Olot's cave. It was a big room with a high, uneven ceiling. Although the walls and floor were stone, Chancy had made it cozy with colorful rugs and soft cushions on the chairs and sofas. Fairy lights made the room bright and inviting.

Blue had scarcely entered the room when the other members of Zephyr came to greet him. Skippy the satyr was the first to say hello, while his two girlfriends giggled behind him. Cheeble, the brownie and professional gambler, didn't say much, but he did give Blue a low five. Blue knew Cory's good friend Daisy, who gave him a hug and a peck on the cheek. The last one to come up was Perky, who had long been one of Santa's elves. He shook Blue's hand before returning to his bells.

Blue seemed more relaxed when he finally sat down on a chair beside Chancy. Cory smiled, grateful that her friends had gone out of their way to welcome him. After doing her wrist exercises, she did a quick tattoo to start her warm-up. It wasn't long before Olot stood and waved his hand to get their attention.

"We have a lot of work ahead of us, and we need to get started," he announced. "We wrote this song in the beginning of the summer, so you may not remember it very well. If you'll recall, we named it 'Summer Heat.' Let's see what we can do with it."

In only moments, Cory was so caught up in the music that she lost track of everything else. She picked up the beat with her drums easily, setting the tempo for the rest of the band. When Olot finally announced that they were done for the night, she was amazed to see how much time had passed.

"Before you go, I have two announcements to make," Olot declared. "As you all know, Goldilocks has married Prince Rupert. She didn't work as my assistant for long, but she was good at what she did. Chancy and I think we need someone to take over her job. If you know of anyone who might be interested, please have them contact me. And that brings me to my second announcement. One of the reasons we feel we need someone in Goldilocks's old position is that Chancy and I are expecting and could use the help."

"Expecting what?" asked Cheeble. "A lot of job applicants?"

"He means they're expecting a baby!" Daisy cried. "Chancy, that's wonderful!"

As everyone started talking at once, Cory and Daisy hurried over to congratulate their friends. Chancy was blushing when they hugged her, and Olot was smiling so broadly that Cory could see every one of his sharp teeth. With all the excitement, it took a while before everyone said good night and left. When they finally did, Cory's mouth was tired from smiling.

"So, what did you think?" she asked Blue as they climbed on his solar cycle.

"I like them a lot," he said, handing her a helmet. "They're almost more like a family than a band."

"And they're my family, which means you'll always be welcome," said Cory. "Especially since you're the best trumpet player around!"

CHAPTER
3

The next day, Cory learned another thing about ogres: they liked to start their parties early. After Blue contacted him, Macks came back to the house to help carry the pies to the park pavilion that the ogres had reserved. They were there by nine in the morning and found that nearly everyone else had already arrived. It was a large park with separate areas set aside for big groups. The pavilion at one end of their area was big enough to seat fifty ogres. A small forest backed the large, flat field where ogres were already drawing lines with chalk.

As soon as they arrived, Blue took Cory around to introduce her to more of his friends. She had seen many of them before, but it was nice to be able to attach names to faces. Although being the only one there without a drop of ogre blood made her uncomfortable at first, everyone was friendly and she soon felt as if she belonged.

They hadn't been there long before the ogres started a game of kick boulder. Blue found a strong branch on a tree at the forest's edge where he and Cory could watch without ogres running over them or flying boulders crushing them. Cory thought it was fun until a boulder to the head knocked out a snaggle-toothed ogre.

"It happens nearly every game," said Blue. "That's usually how they know the game is over."

"Is he going to be all right?" Cory asked as they carried the ogre off the field.

"He'll be fine," Blue told her. "Ogres have very hard heads. See, he's already better."

The injured ogre was struggling against his friends who were carrying him. They dropped him, laughing as he got to his feet and staggered to a nearby bench.

"Now what?" Cory asked as ogres began to gather around a long table.

"Food-eating contest," Blue declared. "No ogre party is complete without a contest where ogres gorge themselves. We'll have to go closer to see what they're eating."

He helped her out of the tree and led her through the crowd until they were standing in front of the table. The ogres made good-natured comments about letting "the shorty" see and gave her the best place to stand. Fourteen ogres and ogresses had taken seats on the opposite side of the table. The noise up close was awful when the contestants began to shout and slam their fists on the table until someone started passing out the food. Cory saw cabbage, both cooked and raw; broccoli; and all sorts of beans passing the length of the table.

"Uh-oh," Blue said in her ear. "That means they're holding a flatulence contest later."

"That's one contest I don't want to be around!" said Cory.

When each ogre had a pile of food, someone rang a bell and they all started stuffing the food into their mouths. The crowd roared in appreciation, urging on their favorites. Cory had to stick her fingers in her ears to make the racket more bearable. Although she thought it was disgusting at first as the ogres crammed more food into their mouths than they could reasonably chew, she soon thought the expressions on their faces were funny and began to laugh along with the rest of the audience.

It wasn't long before they'd eaten more than a fairy could have managed. Soon after that they'd eaten more than a human could have force-fed himself. Cory couldn't believe how much they ate and was feeling slightly queasy when first one, then another gave up. When only one ogre was left, the audience clapped and roared and stomped their feet until the ground shook, and Cory wondered if her hearing might be permanently damaged.

As the noise died down, one ogre raised his voice louder than the others. "Watching them eat has made me hungry. Bring on the food!"

"He's kidding, right?" Cory asked Blue as the crowd headed toward the pavilion where the food had been laid out on tables.

"Not at all," said Blue. "Ogres' three favorite things are eating, drinking, and contests. You're going to see plenty of all three today."

"What about music?" Cory asked him. "They did invite you here to play your trumpet."

Blue grinned. "That's when they'll do their drinking. They'll roll out the barrels of cider once the contests are over."

"What is there to eat?" Cory asked, crinkling her nose at the strange smells.

"Lots of things!" said Blue. "Why don't I get you a plate of food you can eat? It can get pretty rough when a crowd of ogres are vying for their favorites."

Cory took a seat at one of the picnic tables while Blue went to get their lunch. Although the table was empty when she sat, ogres carrying loaded plates soon headed her way. She was glad when Macks took the seat across from her.

"Great party, huh?" he said as he set his plate on the table.

Cory nodded. "It's not like any party I've ever attended before."

"You should enter the next contest," said Macks. "It's a three-legged race. No boulders to roll over you in that one!"

"I'll see," said Cory, not sure she wanted to take part in any ogre contests.

She looked up when Blue sat down beside her. "Here you go," he said. "Corn fritters, turnip greens, and applesauce."

"I'm surprised they have food like this," said Cory.

"Ogres like all sorts of food," Blue told her.

"Don't you eat meat?" asked Macks. "There's some tasty beef and sausages on the end table. They always get the best liverwurst."

Cory shook her head. "My mother is a fairy and I grew up eating like one. Very few fairies eat meat."

"Huh," grunted Macks. "Takes all sorts. Hey, Estel! Over here!" Turning back to Cory, he gestured to the young ogress approaching the table. "That's my girlfriend, Estel. We've been together about a year now."

Cory watched Estel cross the lawn, waving to some ogres, saying hello to others. If she had been a human or fairy, she would have been considered extremely unattractive with her patchy hair, eyes that were two different sizes, lumpy nose, and no chin. But if Macks was indeed considered to be a handsome ogre, she was probably thought to be lovely.

When Estel reached them, Macks scooted over and patted the bench beside him. "Have a seat, sweetie pie. I want you to meet Cory, Blue's girl."

"Hey there," Estel said as she set down her plate. "I'm glad I finally get to meet you. I've heard so much about you from Blue and Macks. I'd be jealous if you weren't so . . . well, you know."

Cory glanced at Blue with one eyebrow raised. He shrugged and patted her hand.

"Cory and I were just talking about the three-legged contest," said Macks. "Why don't you be her partner, Estel? You're closer to her in size than Blue is."

"Sure, I could do that," Estel told him, giving Cory a condescending smile.

When Macks and Estel started their own conversation, Cory whispered to Blue, "What was that all about?"

Blue cleared his throat and looked uncomfortable. "To most other people, you are considered to be a truly beautiful young lady, but ogres have a different standard of beauty. I hate to say this, but she's acting like she feels sorry for you. Estel is a very popular girl among ogres. She thinks she'll be doing you a favor by being your partner in the contest."

"But I don't even want to be in the contest!" said Cory. "I never said I would do it."

"I know," said Blue, "but you sort of have to now. It would be a real insult if you didn't take her up on her offer."

Cory sighed. She'd do it if she had to, but she wasn't looking forward to it. While the ogres gobbled their food, she started picking at her lunch. After the first few bites she discovered that it was surprisingly good. Her appetite had come back, so she ate everything on her plate and sat back to wait for Blue to finish.

"Want to go for a walk?" he asked when he finally set down his fork.

"I'd love to," Cory said.

"Be back in time for the race!" Macks told them as they got up from the table.

"We will," Blue assured him, taking Cory by the arm.

Cory waited until they were alone before saying, "You do realize that Estel may be smaller than you or Macks, but she's still much taller than me and has to weigh at least two hundred pounds more. I don't know if I can do a three-legged race with her."

"You'll be fine," said Blue. "If she has to, she can carry you. After all, you are as light as a feather."

Cory gasped when he swept her off her feet and ran toward the forest. She thought she saw someone dart behind a tree, but then Blue twirled her around and she forgot all about it. Around and around they went until they were both dizzy. When he finally set her down, they leaned against each other, laughing as they waited for the world to stop spinning.

"You know I love you, right?" he murmured into her hair.

"I love you more!" she replied.

"That's not possible," he said.

Blue was about to kiss her when they heard Macks yelling. "Hey, you two lovebirds, the contest is about to start!"

"Rain check?" Blue asked her.

"You'd better believe it!" Cory told him.

Estel was waiting with a length of rope in her hands when Cory and Blue reached the spot where the contest was about to begin. Macks and Blue paired off while the ogress tied her right leg to Cory's left. Someone had used chalk to draw a line on the grass. When all the contestants stood behind it, an ogre standing to the side roared, "Go!" and they all took off.

Cory had been in three-legged races before, but never with an ogress for a partner. She felt like a fly riding on a unicorn's back and had about as much control. She held on to Estel so she wouldn't fall, although the ogress was holding on to her so hard that falling might not have been an option. Estel dragged her down the field, moving her legs at a normal run—for her. To Cory, each ground-pounding step was too fast and jarring, shaking her so that she had to clamp her mouth shut so she wouldn't bite her tongue.

When they rounded the turn in second place, Estel grumbled, "We can do better than this," and started to go faster.

Cory groaned, wondering how she'd ever make it to the end. From what she'd seen of the course, there were two more turns and a long straightaway. They were in the lead when she saw the next turn located by the edge of the trees where she and Blue had almost kissed. Cory and Estel were nearly there when a figure ran out and raised her hand, making the air sparkle in front of her. A moment later the figure turned and ran off, leaving the ground behind her sparkling.

"Estel!" Cory shouted, wanting to warn her partner. When she glanced up, she saw that Estel was looking the other way.

"Macks and Blue are getting close," the ogress panted. "We can't let them catch up. We're almost—"

As they reached the sparkle-covered ground and their feet slid out from under them, Cory realized that it was frost. And then they landed and she felt a bolt of pain shoot through her ankle.

"Watch out!" Blue shouted behind them.

And then Blue and Macks plowed into them and tripped, sprawling on the ground half on top of Cory and Estel. Much to Cory's relief, the next pair of three-legged runners was able to go around them, so no one else joined the pile of bodies.

"Ow!" howled Estel. "Get off me!"

Macks and Blue struggled to stand, although it wasn't easy on the slippery ground, especially when they were still tied together. A crowd had gathered around them by the time Estel and Cory were able to sit up. Macks had untied himself from Blue and was hovering around the edge of the ice when the ogress reached for the rope tying her to Cory.

"Cory, are you okay?" asked Blue.

Cory shook her head. "I think I twisted my ankle."

"Let me help you up," Blue said.

"What about you, sugar lump?" Macks asked Estel.

"I'm fine," she grumbled. "Just mad, that's all. Did anyone see who did this?"

The ogres were shaking their heads when Cory spoke up. "I did. It was a frost fairy. I saw her come out of those trees," she said, pointing.

"The guilds have brought their feud here, to one of *our* parties!" one ogre bellowed.

Estel had untied the rope by the time Blue reached them, so he was able to pick up Cory and carry her back across the frost.

"No one should have been able to do such a thing!" declared one of the largest ogres. "This was our party and Cory is our friend! We're sorry we failed you, Cory. We know all about your campaign against the guilds and we should have protected you better. From now until the trial is over, we'll be watching over you."

"I spent all day yesterday watching over her," Macks told him.

"Yes, but now we'll do it for honor, not money," the bigger ogre told him.

"I thought it was already arranged," Cory whispered to Blue.

"It was, but this is even better," he whispered back. "The ogre who just placed you under the solar-cycle gang's protection is Gnarl, their leader. Now they'll all watch out for you and be more vigilant to gain back the reputation that the frost fairy tarnished. He was right, no one should have been able to do anything to hurt you here."

A roar went up from the three-legged race's finish line, and everyone who had stayed to see about Cory and Estel started heading that way. "It seems the race went on without us," said Cory, wincing when she tried to put her weight on her foot.

"They are ogres," Blue said with a smile. "Are you sure you don't need to see a doctor?"

Cory shook her head. "No, my ankle isn't that bad."

"Do you want to stay at the party or should I take you home?"

"I think I'll be fine as long as I can keep off my foot for a while," said Cory.

"Then how about we have a little music now?" Blue said as he picked her up again.

Cory smiled and settled into his arms. "Sounds good to me!"

After taking Cory to the pavilion and finding her a seat and something to prop up her foot, Blue left to fetch his trumpet from the compartment in his solar cycle. While he was gone, Macks came up to Cory. "Any chance you brought a drum with you?" he asked.

Cory laughed and shook her head. "My drums are a little big to carry on a solar cycle."

"I didn't think you had, but I wanted to ask just in case," he said, and gestured to some other ogres.

The ogres approached Cory then, lugging a trash can and some copper pots. Macks handed her two wooden spoons, saying, "Do you think you can play these instead?"

"I suppose," Cory told him. "It won't sound the same, but I can try."

When Blue came back, he raised his eyebrows when he saw Cory tentatively tapping on the trash can. She shrugged and grinned, saying, "My new drums."

"You don't mind, do you, Blue?" asked Macks. "The boys and I thought she could play along."

"We've never played together before, but I'm sure we can figure something out," said Blue.

While he warmed up, Cory tried to get a feel for her unusual drum set. It wasn't going to be perfect, but then it didn't need to be. Ogres began to gather in the pavilion, talking and laughing until Blue lowered his trumpet and said to Cory, "Do you know 'Midnight Madness'?"

"Sure do," said Cory, and began a drumming introduction. They played then, getting a feel for each other's style. Cory's drum playing was a little rough, but they made do and soon felt as if they had been playing together for ages.

After "Midnight Madness," they played all the songs they both knew that called for a trumpet and drums. It was late afternoon when they finished, tired but happy. When the ogres started to clean up, Blue offered to help, but they turned him down and gave him a generous amount of money for playing. They paid Cory, too, which she wasn't expecting.

Blue and Cory were on their way home before they realized that an ogre was following them. Cory noticed him first. "It's someone from the party," she told Blue. "Should we stop and see what he wants?"

Blue shook his head. "I know what he wants. That's the first bodyguard. Gnarl told me that they're going to take turns."

"He isn't the first," said Cory. "You were the first,

then Macks. Does this mean that I'm going to have a different ogre watching over me every day?"

"Not if it bothers you. I can tell Gnarl that you don't like that if you want me to."

"Please tell him that I'd like Macks to be here most days," said Cory. "He did a good job and I like him."

"I'll talk to Gnarl, but I think the guy following us plans to stick around at least until morning."

Cory sighed. "I hope this trial doesn't last long."

They had almost reached Micah's house when Cory announced, "As soon as we get home, I'm going to take a hot bath and put on comfortable clothes. I'd like to go to bed early tonight."

"Sounds good to me," said Blue. "I can make supper while you relax and—Say, what's that?"

They were still three houses from Micah's, but they could already see that something was wrong. The front yard was covered with frost, making it sparkle just like the patch of ground had sparkled during the race.

"Frost fairies came here, too!" said Cory. "Oh, no! They've frozen all of Uncle Micah's flowers. I bet every one of them is dead."

"It looks as if they were very thorough," Blue said as he got off his solar cycle. "They even froze the flowers in the pot on the porch."

"I'm too tired to deal with this now," Cory told him.

"It can wait," said Blue. "You're still going to take your hot bath and get comfortable. The frost should be gone by morning, and if the flowers are already dead, one more day won't make a difference."

CHAPTER
4

Micah was on his way out the front door the next day when he remembered something. "I forgot to tell you," he said when he returned to the kitchen where Cory, Blue, and the ogre named Snifflit were eating breakfast. Cory's foot was already feeling better after a night of rest. "Yesterday during my planning period, I contacted the Itinerant Troublemakers Guild and filed a complaint about how they sent two members to our house on one night. I know you reported them to the FLEA, Blue, but I wanted the guild to hear that I'm not happy about it. I've taught a lot of their members over the years, so my word might carry a little weight. Don't worry, Cory. I didn't mention your friend, Harmony Twitchet. I know she just came by to warn us that the ITG was going to send its Big Baddies after us."

"Thank you, Uncle Micah," said Cory. "I wouldn't want to get her in trouble when she was trying to be a friend."

"Speaking of friends," Cory said after Micah was gone, "I need to contact Mary Lambkin as soon as I finish eating. I'll start cleaning up the yard after that. Are you going to be staying all day, Snifflit, or is someone else coming over?"

"Snifflit is going to leave when Macks gets here," said Blue. "I contacted Gnarl after you went to bed last night. Macks will be here most days, although Gnarl will send over more ogres if we need them."

"Is Macks taking time off from a job? Is this going to be hard for him?" asked Cory.

"Not at all," said Blue. "He works for his brother in construction. Alecks understands and is fine with it."

"I'm not that lucky," said Snifflit. "I have a job, and I have to go home and change my clothes so I can get to work on time. Do you mind if I don't wait until Macks gets here? As long as you'll still be around, Blue. I don't want to leave Cory on her own."

"No problem," said Blue.

"What kind of job do you have?" Cory asked the ogre.

"I own North Side Beauty Salon," he said as he got up from the table. "My wife and I are both hairdressers there."

"I've heard of that salon. It has a great reputation!" said Cory.

Snifflit shrugged. "What can I say? I'm an artist who happens to work with hair. Thanks for dinner last night and breakfast this morning. I hope you have an uneventful day."

"Thank you for staying," said Cory.

"Yeah, buddy. Thanks!" Blue added.

"Send me a message if you need me again," Snifflit told them as he left.

"He was very nice," Cory said once Snifflit was gone.

"Most ogres are once you get to know them," said Blue.

While Cory finished her breakfast, she wrote the message to Mary Lambkin. She said good-bye to Blue, and he went out on the porch to pet Noodles and wait for Macks while she sent the message.

Mary,

There's someone I'd like you to meet. His name is Jasper Wilkins. I think he would be just right for you. Are you interested?

Cory

"By just right, I mean absolutely perfect," Cory said to herself as she sent the message.

"Were you talking to me?" Macks said as he walked in the door. "Blue just drove off."

Cory laughed. "No, I was sending a message to a friend. Thank you for coming over, Macks. I have to clean up the yard today. The frost fairies paid a visit while we were at the party."

"I saw that," he said. "I can help with the cleanup as long as you tell me what to do with all the dead plants."

Ping! The bell announced the arrival of a message. "I'll be out in just a minute," Cory told Macks. Taking the message from the incoming basket, she opened it and read,

Cory,

My brothers and I are having a housewarming party tomorrow night. We would really like it if you and Blue could be there.

Your friend,
Alphonse Porcine

She had just written back, saying that she and Blue would love to attend the pig brothers' party, when another message arrived.

Cory,

Yes, I'm interested!

Mary

Cory's next message was to Jasper.

Mr. Wilkins,

I am a matchmaker working in the area. I have the perfect match for you! Would you be interested in meeting her?

Corialis Feathering

She waited in the main room, straightening the furniture and cleaning up after the bird that lived on the mantel. If Jasper Wilkins turned her down, she'd have to find another way to bring them together, but this would certainly be the easiest. To her relief, it wasn't long before he sent a message back.

Miss Feathering,

I've heard of you. You made a match for my friend Jack Nimble. I'd be happy to meet the lovely lady you have in mind.

Jasper Wilkins

It took Cory only a few minutes to write messages to

both Mary Lambkin and Jasper Wilkins, setting up the date. Instead of waiting for a reply again, she hurried outside to talk to Macks. She had just told him where to put the dead flowers he'd already dug up when Weegie plopped down by her feet.

"Whatcha doing?" the woodchuck asked.

"We're cleaning up after the latest visit from the frost fairy," said Cory. "Did you or Noodles see them do this yesterday?"

"If we had, we would have stopped them, now, wouldn't we?" Weegie snapped. "We didn't see anything. Noodles and I have been digging a den in your yard. Noodles wants to stay here with you, but I can't sleep in that house anymore. We should be done in a day or two. In the meantime, would you please tell that big guy to stop trying to fill in our hole? It's going to take forever if we have to keep digging it out again."

Cory glanced at Macks. "I'll tell him if you'll tell me something first. Did you ask Micah if you could dig up his yard? This is his house, you know."

"Of course we asked him! It was yesterday morning when he was running down the sidewalk, saying he was late for work. He said, 'Sure, sure. Whatever you need.' He's an awfully accommodating man."

"Somehow I don't think he knew what he was agreeing to. Oh, well. Dig your hole. We can always set a post next to it or plant some flowers around it so people know it's there and don't step in it and get hurt."

"Landscaping! I like it!" said Weegie.

Cory smiled as the woodchuck waddled off. Having a talking animal around certainly was interesting.

Cory and Macks spent the entire morning working in the yard. After digging up the plants, they filled in the holes and raked the dirt smooth. The dead plants went in the compost bin behind the garden shed. When Macks offered to mow the lawn, Cory opened the door to the shed and he got the mower out. Cory cleaned up the dirt they'd spilled while removing the dead plant from the pot on the porch, then decided that the whole porch needed washing. While Macks mowed, Cory scrubbed the porch, including the railings. She was working on the steps when Macks started trimming the tall grass edging the house.

They were both hungry when Cory went inside to get cleaned up and make sandwiches. After lunch, she started a casserole. Zephyr was playing at the Shady Nook that night, so they'd have to eat an early supper. Cory was cleaning up the kitchen when she remembered the messages she'd sent. Two replies were waiting in the basket. Both Mary and Jasper had agreed to the time and place.

Blue was a little late getting home that night, so Cory already had the food on the table when he arrived. Because Macks was going to the Shady Nook with them, they all sat down to eat, saving some of the casserole for Micah, who wasn't home yet. They left soon after that, knowing how hard it was to find solar-cycle parking near the Shady Nook on the nights Zephyr was playing.

People were already lining up outside the restaurant when Cory, Blue, and Macks arrived. Many of them recognized Cory and Blue, and they crowded around, shouting, while Macks tried to make them keep their distance. Although Cory was afraid that some of them might be as unfriendly as the people at the market, she was delighted that they all seemed to be fans.

Once they were inside, Cory sighed with relief. She loved her fans, but the press of people had been frightening. She was glad that Blue and Macks were there, not knowing what she would have done if she'd shown up by herself.

When it occurred to her that some of her bandmates might show up alone, she turned to Macks. "Would you mind standing outside and making sure that the rest of the people in Zephyr can get through the crowd?"

"No problem," said the ogre, and headed back outside.

While Blue found a table near the front of the room, Cory checked on her drums. Olot and Chancy had already brought in all the instruments and had nearly finished setting up everything. Cory was moving a few things when Daisy and Cheeble walked in. Less than a minute later, Daisy came over to talk to her.

"How have you been?" asked Daisy. "Things have been so crazy lately that I haven't had a chance to really talk to you."

"It's been crazy for me, too," Cory said. "The guilds harass me every chance they get."

"What are you doing tomorrow night? Would you and Blue like to come over for supper?"

"That's awfully nice," said Cory, "but we already have plans. The three little pigs are having a housewarming party and invited us."

"That's right!" Daisy said. "They bought Olot's spare cave."

Cory nodded. "I can't wait to see what they did with it."

"Ladies, it's time to warm up," Olot announced.

Cory glanced at the door. Jack Horner had opened it, letting his patrons in. Even though he'd instituted a cover charge when Zephyr played, the restaurant was soon packed.

"I'll talk to you later," Daisy said, and returned to her place on the stage.

Cory picked up her drumsticks and began her warm-up exercises. When they actually began to play, she let herself get immersed in the music. The audience loved "Morning Mist" like they always did.

"And now we'd like to introduce a new song," said Olot. "We wrote it ourselves and named it 'Summer Heat.'"

Cory was surprised. Usually they practiced a song more before they played it in public for the first time. When they started, however, everyone played without any hitches. Like "Morning Mist," a song they had also written, "Summer Heat" seemed to transport the audience to a different time and place. It was a summer day and the sun burned a hole in the sky directly overhead. Hot air shimmered above the baking rocks. Frantic bees buzzed around a patch of wildflowers, rich with heavy perfume. Dried, yellowing grass crunched underfoot. When the music changed, introducing the whisper of a light breeze to cool the air, people in the audience sighed as if they could actually feel it. Leaves rustled in the nearby trees, offering shade. Water gurgled over smooth pebbles in a clear stream, inviting bare feet to dandle and hands to splash. It was a summer that many remembered, and those who didn't wished that they did.

There was magic in the music; everyone could feel it. Cory's grandfather had told her that her Cupid's magic had changed her other songs. She had a feeling that it was true about this one as well.

When the song was over, the crowd stood to applaud, shouting the names of their favorite band members. Apparently, they had liked the new song even more than "Morning Mist." It took a few minutes for the audience to calm down. When they did, Zephyr started to play "June Bug Jamboree," but they had played only a few meters when a woman in the back of the restaurant started to shriek. People turned to look as others began to scream and jump on their chairs.

"Rats!" a man yelled. "There are rats all over the place!"

Cory noticed movement in the rear of the room as three people ran out the door. And then others were getting out of their seats and turning toward the exits. When they started to run, their feet flew out from under them and they landed flat on their backs.

The screaming grew louder as people realized that ice covered the floor and they couldn't leave without risk of falling. Cory could see the rats now, running between the tables and up the backs of chairs. A man threw a salt shaker at a rat, and soon everyone was throwing things at them.

"Quiet!" Olot bellowed, and everyone grew still.

Blue hopped onto the stage beside Olot. "Everyone stay right where you are. I'm FLEA Junior Officer Blue. We need to find out what just happened. First of all, is anyone injured?"

When no one replied, he continued. "Did anyone notice anything suspicious before the rats appeared?"

Everyone looked at everyone else, but no one spoke up.

"Who was the first person to see a rat?" Blue asked.

The woman who had shrieked raised her hand. "I think I did," she said, her voice shaky.

"I saw them, too!" called out another woman.

"So did I!" shouted a man.

"So they started in the back of the room and spread out from there. I know that this restaurant does not have rats, so someone must have brought them in. Did anyone see someone who didn't belong?"

Cory raised her hand. "I saw three people run out the door right after the screaming started."

"I want everyone to look around you. Do you see any empty seats or notice that anyone you saw earlier is missing? Please raise your hand if you do."

No one raised a hand.

"That means that someone came in after the concert started. At least one person brought in rats, and at least one put ice on the floor. Has anyone noticed anything else that was unusual?"

No one answered until a voice called from the floor. "May I get up now?" asked a dwarf who was lying on his back. "This floor is really cold."

Nervous laughter ran through the crowd.

"Everyone, stay where you are until we come help you. We don't want anyone to get hurt," Blue announced before turning to Olot. "We'll start at the back and help them out the door. The rest of the band should stay on the stage for now."

Cory set her drumsticks down. She already knew what had happened and was sure Blue did, too. Fairies from one guild or another had brought rats to the restaurant. A frost fairy had frozen the floor. It was all because she was there, playing the drums. The fairies weren't going to let her go one day without doing something to plague her. She was just surprised that they had done it in such a public place with so many people present.

The members of Zephyr packed up their instruments while Blue, Olot, Jack Horner, and his waiters helped the patrons across the slippery floor and out the door. It was a long, slow process, made messier as the ice began to melt. A shape-shifter in the audience volunteered to catch the rats, but Jack Horner asked him to wait until all the paying customers were gone. When the last one had reached the door, the shape-shifter turned into a bobcat and began to chase the rats, devouring each one he caught.

There was nothing but water on the floor when Blue said that the band members could go. Cory stayed by her drums while Blue and Olot talked to Jack Horner.

"You know I can't pay you for tonight," Jack told Olot. "I had to offer refunds to anyone who asked, and now I have to pay for the damage. Look at my floors! There are scratch marks on chairs and tables where the rats climbed them. *And* I'll have to hire an exterminator to get rid of the rats that cat guy doesn't catch."

"I understand," said Olot.

"By all accounts, you should send the bill to the guilds that did the damage," Blue told him. "We know that at least one frost fairy was here, and possibly one or two members of another guild. I'm going to investigate. I'll let you know what I find out."

"You do that," said Jack Horner. "But I can tell you right now, I won't be asking Zephyr to play here again. Or in any of my other restaurants. Not as long as this kind of thing might happen."

Although Cory wanted to say something to Olot as he started carrying the instruments to his cart, she saw the look on his face and didn't dare. "Wait a few days," Blue told her when he saw the way she was watching Olot. "He might be ready to talk to you by then."

CHAPTER
5

Cory didn't sleep well that night. It had occurred to her that she should quit Zephyr so they could play without the guilds' interference. But she loved playing with the band and knew she would feel like a part of her was missing if she quit. She was making money by playing the drums, too, which was a big help now that she couldn't do odd jobs. Wondering how much more of her life the guilds were going to ruin, she fell into a troubled sleep and woke in a bad mood.

She didn't say much to Blue or Micah at breakfast, and fed Noodles and Weegie without a word. When Macks arrived, she still didn't have much to say. Remembering that she and Blue were supposed to go to the pigs' party that night, she wondered if she should try to get out of it, but couldn't think of a good enough reason.

It occurred to her that if they were going, she'd have to get the pigs a housewarming gift. That meant a trip to the market, yet another thing that she didn't feel like doing. If she did go, she didn't want to be recognized, especially after what had happened last time.

Cory was trying to think of a way to change her appearance that didn't look fake or silly, when a message arrived in the basket.

Miss Feathering,

I am the Prosecuting Law Upholder in the case *People versus Guilds*. As such, I need to meet with you. Are you available this morning?

Natinia Blunk

Why not? Cory thought, and sent a message back asking what time she would like to meet. She turned around in surprise when there was a knock at the door.

"I'll get that," said Macks, looking grim. "Stay back in case it's someone from a guild."

Cory stood in the entrance to the hallway leading to the bedrooms so she could run into one if necessary. She watched as Macks opened the door, straining to listen to his conversation. Whoever had come to the door was very soft-spoken. Cory could hear only Macks's side of the conversation, which consisted mostly of "Yeah" and "Uh-huh."

"Who is it, Macks?" Cory finally asked him.

"She says her name is Natinia Blunk," Macks said, opening the door wide.

Cory blinked in surprise. "That was fast."

Natinia slipped her small, portable message sender back into her purse and looked up at Cory. The woman barely came up to Cory's waist, and was very well dressed in a stylish blue suit. The biggest surprise was that she was a goblin. Cory had never spoken to a female goblin before. Most goblins believed that their women should stay at home and not work outside the house. Obviously, Natinia didn't feel that way.

"You said you could meet, so I thought, why not now?" Natinia said in a soft, sweet voice that didn't go with her lumpy goblin nose and sharply pointed ears that stuck out through her carefully styled hair. "I was in the area anyway, but I didn't want to stop by without giving you some warning. May I come in?"

"Oh my, yes! Please do," Cory told her, walking into the main room. "Would you like to sit down?"

"Yes, thank you. These shoes are new and aren't broken in yet. I'm happy for any excuse to sit. So, Miss Feathering—"

"You can call me Cory."

"I'll be outside," said Macks. "Holler if you need me."

Natinia smiled as the door shut behind the ogre. "All right, Cory. It sounds as if you have a real grievance against the Tooth Fairy Guild, the Flower Fairy Guild, the Frost Fairy Guild, the Itinerant Troublemakers Guild, and the Housecleaning Guild. Have I left anyone out?"

"The Sandman Guild," said Cory. "One of their members came by the house two nights in a row, even though my uncle had filled out a do-not-visit form."

"Ah, yes. I see that's listed here. Would you mind telling me in your own words how these guilds harassed you?"

"Not at all," said Cory. "It started when I quit the Tooth Fairy Guild." She told the woman everything, from the day she quit the guild, to the day the guild locked her in a glass cylinder and took away her fairy abilities, including her fairy wings. She told Natinia of all the awful things the various guilds had done since then, right up to bringing the rats and freezing the floor at the Shady Nook the night before. The only part she left out was her discovery that she was a Cupid and the job that came with it.

Natinia wrote everything down, nodding now and then, and saying "Oh my!" or "They didn't!" in such a soft voice that Cory almost didn't hear her. When Cory was finished, Natinia set down her ink stick and leaned back in the chair.

"I know you told most of this to the big jury," said Natinia, "but I wanted to hear it for myself. The harassment doesn't seem to have stopped, does it?"

"Not at all," said Cory.

"Well, then, it's time we did something about it. You are going to be called to testify at court tomorrow. I will be there asking questions, and so will the attorney representing the guilds. Be forewarned, their attorney will not be nice. He will try to pick apart your story or get you so confused that you contradict yourself. Don't let him do this. Be calm, and don't let his little games rattle you. Remember this and I'm sure you'll be fine."

"You just made me a whole lot more nervous than I was before," Cory said with a little laugh.

"Better warned than taken by surprise," Natinia said as she gathered her belongings. "I'll see you at court tomorrow."

"She seemed nice!" Macks said when Natinia was gone.

"You sound as if you didn't expect her to be nice," said Cory.

"I didn't! She's a goblin. They're never nice."

"Have you ever met a female goblin before?" Cory asked him.

"Never," Macks said. "And I don't know anyone who has. Until now, I guess."

Resigned to going to the party and buying a gift to take, Cory asked Macks to get ready, then went to her room to look for a disguise. When she couldn't find anything better, she twisted her hair into a bun and put on a pair of dark glasses. "I hope this is enough," she said, checking herself in a mirror.

She was on her way out the door when she thought about the goblin woman. "She's the kind of person that grumpy goblin Officer Deeds should marry," she murmured to herself.

Cory was picturing the goblin officer when another face popped into her head. Normally this meant that her Cupid abilities were working and the second person was the first one's true love. Cory gasped, hoping this wasn't true. The second person was her mother, Delphinium.

Cory had matched up a number of couples. Some were her friends and some were strangers. Some she was happy to match, while she wasn't so sure about others. Cory had really struggled with whether or not she should match Goldilocks with the already engaged Prince Rupert. She had decided to follow her Cupid instincts only after she saw how right they were for each other. But she couldn't imagine matching her mother with that horrible goblin officer! She'd met Officer Deeds only a few times; he always seemed to enjoy being nasty. Cory and her mother hadn't gotten along for ages and it had only gotten worse after Cory quit the Tooth Fairy Guild. The last time she saw Delphinium, her mother had disowned her, which had been a relief for Cory. It meant that her mother no longer stopped by to berate her. True, her mother and Deeds were both unpleasant people, but wouldn't they get worse if they were together? The thought of matching them up made Cory shudder. "I am not going to do that!" she muttered.

Cory didn't realize that she had said it out loud until Macks said, "Do what?"

"Oh, nothing," she replied.

Very few people knew that Cory was a Cupid. Her grandfather Lionel was one as well, and he had told her that her job would be much easier if people didn't know. The only other people who knew were those she really trusted, like Blue, her uncle Micah, and the putti who worked for her grandfather. Her friend Marjorie

Muffet knew because Cory had told her before Lionel suggested that it should be a secret, but Marjorie didn't believe her. Cory didn't know Macks well enough to tell him, which meant that she'd have to be more careful when he was around.

"Are you ready to go?" asked Macks.

Cory slung her purse over her shoulder. "I suppose it would be too much to ask if we could try to be inconspicuous?"

"Huh?" said Macks.

"Never mind," she said, wishing they didn't have to go anywhere.

Instead of heading for one of the big markets, Cory had Macks take her to a street not far from Perfect Pastry. While visiting the pastry shop once, she had noticed a home furnishings store nearby. Before she even entered the store, she had a good idea what she wanted.

Cory didn't know a lot about the three little pigs, but she did know that they liked to wallow in the oversize bathtub in the back of their cave. She'd also heard that they had already filled it with mud. When she entered the shop, she headed straight for the clocks. It was easy enough to lose track of time when one took a bath. Cory thought it would be even easier for a pig who was lying in a tub of mud.

Cory was looking at a fancy clock showing the four seasons when a salesman approached her. "May I help you?" he asked.

"Yes, please," said Cory. "I'm looking for a clock that will hold up to moisture and mud."

"Ah!" said the salesman, and he turned to face the clocks. "I'm sure I have the right clock for you." The first clock he showed her was very beautiful. "The face of this clock is made from crystal from Mount Elva. The clock can announce the correct time out loud in any of the fey languages. The owner need only choose. It is impervious to any liquid, including the stomach acid of a roc."

"I don't think . . . ," Cory began.

"This clock tells the time in every fey city," he said, gesturing to the next clock over. Dozens of tiny clocks ringed the large clock in the center. "It can withstand the pressure of the deep sea, and would be an excellent gift for a mermaid."

"It's not for a mermaid," Cory told him.

"Well, then, you might prefer this beauty," he said, walking her to a clock on a pedestal by itself. "It tells the time in the human and fey worlds simultaneously, which is no mean feat considering that the rate that time passes in the two worlds often varies. We've been in a most unusual period where the two times coincide, but that won't last for long, I assure you. When it begins fluctuating again, this clock will be extremely useful for those who pass between the worlds. It is also impervious to anything, including lava. I'd have to say that this is the most extraordinary clock in the store."

Macks whistled, long and low. "And the most expensive," he said, eyeing the price tag.

"The elves made this clock, so of course it's infused with their magic," the salesman said, sounding as if he'd been personally offended. "The price reflects that, too, of course."

"Don't you have anything simpler and less expensive?" Cory asked.

"Oh, you want to go in that direction!" the salesman said, his gaze turning scornful. "Over here, we have a waterproof clock that tells the time. I think it's boring and unattractive, but if that's what you want . . ."

"I'll take it!" Cory told him. It was an ordinary clock without any fancy, unnecessary flourishes, which was all the pigs needed.

"Then I'll get it wrapped for you," the salesman told her, his look saying that Cory was just as boring and unattractive as the clock.

This delighted Cory, because it meant that the

salesman hadn't recognized her. Apparently, the bun and dark glasses had worked!

Cory was quite pleased with her purchase when they left the store. While she waited for Macks to put the clock in the cycle compartment, she noticed that no one walking past spared her a second glance. She was in a good mood when they climbed onto the ogre's solar cycle and started down the road. But then she saw a sign posted on a streetlamp.

CORY FEATHERING HATES FAIRIES!

"That's not true!" she said as they sped past. "I'm half fairy myself!"

The next sign was worse.

STOP CORY FEATHERING BEFORE SHE DESTROYS THE GUILDS.

"But that's not at all—"

And then she saw that all the streetlamps bore signs, and they were all about her.

THE GUILDS ARE ON YOUR SIDE. CORY FEATHERING ISN'T!

**SAY YES TO GUILDS! SAY NO TO
CORY FEATHERING!
THE GUILDS HAVE RIGHTS, TOO!
STOP CORY FEATHERING.**

By the time Macks turned off the main road and
headed toward Micah's house, Cory was close to tears.

CHAPTER
6

*C*ory and Macks spent a quiet afternoon inside. Cory read a book, then took a nap, thinking that maybe she was feeling so low because she was tired. Macks left when Blue showed up, and for once the ogre seemed relieved to go.

It was early evening when Cory and Blue left the house on their way to the three little pigs' cave. There was a slight chill to the air, a reminder that autumn was about to arrive. When they reached the cave, Blue parked his solar cycle halfway down the path that concealed the cave door from the road. They didn't hear a sound from inside the cave until Alphonse opened the door, and then music and laughter poured out, welcoming them to the party.

"I'm glad you could make it!" Alphonse shouted over the noise. "Come on in. I believe you know just about everybody."

"We brought you a housewarming gift. Where should we put it?" Cory said, holding up the wrapped clock.

"Thank you!" said Alphonse, looking very pleased. "I'll put it on the gift table with the others."

From the noise coming out of the main room, Cory expected a big crowd, but there really weren't that many people. Olot and Chancy were sitting in the middle of the room with everyone gathered around listening to the ogre strum his lute. Cory's neighbor the witch Wanita, had brought her pet boar, Boris, who was happily eating from a big bowl placed on the floor. Alphonse's two brothers, Roger and Bertie, were offering trays laden down with drinks. Cory was surprised to see that her grandfather Lionel was there talking to a female pig in a pretty silk dress.

"We asked Olot to bring his lute," Alphonse told Cory. "He's very good, isn't he?"

"Yes, he is," Cory said, smiling. She had always enjoyed Olot's solos and was happy to hear him play again. It seemed to make him happy, too, because he had his eyes closed and was wearing a faint smile as he played. Cory hoped this meant that he was no longer upset about what had happened at the Shady Nook. But then he looked up and saw Cory and his smile faded.

Cory was talking to Alphonse and Blue when Olot finished the song. Excusing himself from the people around him, he headed over to Cory.

She stepped aside, hoping to keep their conversation private. "I wanted to talk to you after what happened last night," said Olot. "You were there when Jack Horner told me that he didn't want us playing at his restaurants anymore. Apparently, no other restaurant owners do, either. I got messages today from all of them. They don't want us back until the trial is over."

"I'm so sorry," Cory told him. "I wanted to talk to you about that, too. I've been thinking, and I've decided that I should quit Zephyr, at least for now. It's my fault that the guilds did those things last night. If I weren't part of the band, none of that would have happened."

Olot looked horrified. "You can't mean it! Zephyr needs you, Cory! No one wants you to leave. Not only are you the best drummer around, but our songs have been so much better ever since you started helping us write them. You're an important part of the band! You don't really want to leave, do you?"

Cory shook her head. "Not at all, but you shouldn't have to deal with this."

"And neither should you," said Olot. "We'll stand by you just as we know you'd stand by us. Zephyr isn't just the instruments or the music. The people in it are equally important. I do have some good news, though. We have one booking. My third cousin, four times removed, wants Zephyr to play at his birthday party. He sent me a message this morning. We're playing for him three days from today. He's very excited."

"Was it Itchy Butt?" asked Cory. "He told me he wanted Zephyr to play for him."

Olot nodded. "Itchy Butt told me that he knows other family members who are interested, too. So even if we won't be playing in restaurants, we're still going to get some gigs."

"That's wonderful!" said Cory. "It's the best news I've heard in a while."

A bell rang, drawing everyone's attention to Alphonse. "Dinner is ready! We're having a buffet, so please get in line and help yourselves."

"Is everything all right?" Blue asked Cory as they got behind Wanita.

Cory nodded. "Better than I thought."

"Isn't this a nice party?" Wanita said to them. "Boris,

stop chewing on that chair! I'll get you more food in just a minute. People will think you've never been to a party before!"

The boar grunted and started snuffling at a sofa cushion.

"Actually, the only parties he's ever attended were the ones my sister witches put on and they had their pets there, too. He's never been to a pig party before, but then neither have I. What do you suppose they're serving?" She leaned forward, trying to see around Olot and Chancy. "It looks like a lot of corn dishes. Good, Boris will like that!"

Wanita was right. When it was their turn to serve themselves, Cory saw that everything was corn related. The first platter held corn on the cob. After that she saw corn dogs, corn bread, corn pudding, and corn chowder. Cory wondered how they were going to work the drinks into the corn menu and was relieved to find apple cider.

Carrying plates piled high with food, Cory and Blue found some small, round chairs shaped like apples grouped together in a corner. A few minutes later Lionel joined them, taking the third chair. Cory giggled when she saw the refined gentleman sitting on a giant apple with his plate balanced on his lap.

He gave her a wry smile when he saw that she was laughing. "I wasn't sure what to expect when I accepted the pigs' invitation, but it wasn't this. I met them at your party. I must admit that I never expected to see them again."

"They're very nice, especially Alphonse," said Cory. "I have to say, they've done a lovely job with the cave."

"I like the walls," said Blue.

"The stripes are very nice," agreed Cory's grandfather. "Are they natural?"

Cory nodded. "I saw the cave before the pigs moved in. The stripes are layers of different kinds of rock. I like the way the pigs picked up the colors in their furnishings. It's a big cave, but they've made it look cozy and inviting."

"That reminds me of a proposal I have for you," said Lionel. "As you know, my house is very large, certainly too large for just one person. I was wondering if you'd like to move in with me. You could have the pick of the spare bedrooms and there's plenty of room behind the house for your woodchucks. You'd be doing an old man a big favor. It would be nice to have company so I'm not rattling around in the house by myself."

"But the putti live there, don't they? You aren't really alone," said Cory.

"That's true, but as wonderful as they are, it just isn't the same as having a real member of my family in the house. And just think, Blue and the other bodyguards wouldn't have to sleep on the floor in the main room."

"I must admit, that is a wonderful invitation and very tempting, but I'm happy where I am," said Cory. "Uncle Micah and I have a comfortable relationship, and I don't want to desert him."

"I can understand that," said her grandfather, "but will you at least give my offer some consideration?"

"Of course!" said Cory. "I promise."

When they'd finished eating, Blue and Cory wandered around, talking to everyone at the party and enjoying Olot's music when the pigs convinced him to play again. The pigs gave everyone a tour of the cave after that, including the huge bathing room and the shallow pool filled with liquid mud. When they returned to the main room, there was cake to eat and presents for the pigs to open. The three little pigs loved the clock that Cory had picked out, and the candlesticks that Lionel had brought. Olot and Chancy had given them a vegetable steamer, which the pigs vowed to use the very next day. Petal, the female pig, had given them dish towels and an apron. Cory had figured out that Petal was Alphonse's girlfriend, so she wasn't surprised when she heard Petal say that part of her gift was to come over and make the three pigs supper one night soon.

"That's good," declared Roger. "That apron won't fit any of us. The only one it will fit is you, Petal."

The little sow smiled and flushed bright pink. Cory guessed that Petal really had bought it for herself.

When the three brothers unwrapped the gift from Wanita, they couldn't help showing their disappointment. "Oh, it's a candle," said Alphonse. "How very nice."

"It's not just a candle," said Wanita. "I made it myself. You light it in one room and all the insects in your house will leave. I have one just like it at home. I started using mine over the summer when Boris got extra stinky and attracted lots of flies. I put magic in it, you know."

"The candle should be very useful," said Alphonse, although he looked a little doubtful. "Thank you all for your marvelous gifts. They'll make our house even more special."

Everyone admired the gifts for a time, but it wasn't long before Blue said to Cory, "Are you ready to go?"

"Getting bored, huh?" Cory whispered.

"You know it," said Blue. "But that's not all. You're going to have a very busy day tomorrow. You might want to get to bed earlier than usual."

"We're going to head home, too," said Olot when he saw Chancy yawning.

After saying good-bye to everyone, the two couples left the cave together. Olot and Chancy took a shortcut to their own cave, while Cory and Blue started down the main path, looking for Blue's solar cycle. Blue was getting the helmets out of the compartment when a sound overhead made them both look up. Dozens of tiny fairies were flying above them, their frantically beating wings creating a flickering light. They were carrying the bags that tooth fairies used to carry the teeth they collected. From what Cory could see, the bags were heavy enough to be full.

Blue started to call out just as the fairies dumped the contents of their bags. Diseased teeth from every race and species showered down on Cory and Blue. Familiar with teeth, Cory knew what they were right away, and shrieked in anger and surprise. She wrapped her arms around her head to protect her face.

"What are these things?" Blue roared, pulling his shirt over his head to cover it.

"Bad teeth," said Cory. "I'd know that awful smell anywhere!"

"What's wrong?" Olot bellowed, running back down the shortcut. "Is someone hurt?"

"No," Cory said as the fairies flew off. "Just mad. Did you see the bags they were carrying? Once a tooth fairy gets a bag for the teeth they collect, they never loan them or give them to anyone. There's no doubt about it. Those were tooth fairies. Yuck! I hate the smell of rotting teeth!"

"What they did wasn't nice, but at least no one was hurt," said Olot.

"They weren't trying to hurt us, just show me how much they hate me," said Cory. "They had to take off from work to do this, and now they'll have to go home and wash those tooth bags. The fact that they touched those teeth at all says a lot. Tooth fairies hate rotting teeth and don't want anything to do with them. As far as they're concerned, dumping those teeth on us was the ultimate insult."

"I'm sure you're right," said Blue, "but like Olot said, it could have been worse. Let's get to Micah's house before anything else happens."

Olot started back toward his cave as Cory and Blue took off on the solar cycle. Cory was thinking about a hot bath and bed when suddenly Blue jerked the cycle hard to the right and they skidded off the road, landing in the underbrush. Cory flew off the cycle and into a shrub headfirst, collecting cuts and scratches on the way.

Her ears rang from the awful screech of the tires on the road, yet Blue's bellow was so loud that she could still hear him. "Cory, are you all right?" he cried as she struggled to pull herself out of the shrub.

"I'll tell you in a minute," she said. "I seem to be stuck."

"I'll get those blasted fairies!" Blue roared as he began ripping chunks of the shrub out of the way in an effort to reach Cory.

Something crashed down the mountainside, coming directly at them. Blue stopped breaking the shrub. A moment later, Cory heard him telling Olot what had happened. Then they were both working on the shrub and she was out a few seconds later.

"We're going to have to do something about that hole," Blue told Olot. "The pedal-bus could come along at any time and a lot of people could get hurt."

"What hole?" Cory asked.

"The hole someone dug in the middle of the road," Blue said, pointing. "I turned when I did so we wouldn't fall in."

Cory strode to the edge of the road to peer into the hole. In the moonlight, it looked like a dark patch in the middle of the road. Bending down to get a closer look, she rested her hand on the ground. The dirt was crumbly and broke apart under her weight. "It looks freshly dug," she said. "And it smells like fertilizer."

"Flower fairies probably did it," said Blue. "They always put fertilizer in the bottoms of the holes they dig when they're planting something. It's the only kind of holes they know how to dig. They must have done it after we went past on our way to the party."

"They dumped the dirt over here," Olot told them from the other side of the road.

"I'm sure it's no coincidence that it happened tonight," Blue told Cory. "Everyone knows that you're scheduled to testify tomorrow."

"I'll get some shovels so we can fill in the hole," said Olot, turning toward his cave.

"And I'll make sure no one is coming this way, so we can warn them off," said Cory. "We don't want anyone falling in. I can't believe the guilds did this. It's so dangerous! Someone could have been seriously hurt."

"I think that was the guilds' intention," Blue said. "My guess is that someone told a guild member that we were going to be here tonight. Tooth fairies don't fly around lugging rotting teeth without a reason. I don't know who dug that hole, but I'm sure it was done for us. I know I didn't mention this party to anyone. Did you?"

Cory thought long and hard. Who had she seen recently that she could have told? It was only yesterday that the pigs invited them. She'd seen Blue and Micah and Macks, but they didn't count. And then she remembered her short conversation with Daisy.

"I told Daisy!" said Cory. "Last night before the performance. She invited us to supper tonight, and I said we couldn't come because the three pigs had invited us to a party. I'm sure she's the only one."

"Then she's the one we need to see about this," Blue told her. "I want to know who she told before you go to court tomorrow. Did she report it directly to her guild? She is a flower fairy, isn't she? I need to find out what else she's been telling them."

Cory shook her head. She couldn't believe that Daisy would ever betray her. "Daisy is a member of the Flower Fairy Guild, but she would never turn on me that way. She's been my friend for most of my life."

"We'll see," said Blue. "As we all know, guilds can be very persuasive."

⫸→

It didn't take long for Olot and Blue to fill in the hole in the road. When they left, Blue headed straight for Daisy's parents' house. "It's late for a flower fairy to be up," Cory told him. "She probably went to bed hours ago."

"Then her parents will have to get her out of bed," said Blue. "This is important."

Cory touched the side of her face and winced. It had been dark when they had their near-accident and Blue hadn't gotten a good look at her yet. Although she hadn't been badly hurt, some of her cuts had bled a lot. She was afraid that when he did see her, he was going to be even angrier at Daisy.

The house was dark when they reached it. Blue parked his solar cycle by the front walk and hurried to the porch. He was rapping at the door with his knuckles when Cory joined him. "They've probably all gone to bed," she told him.

"Then they'll have to get up," said Blue. "I'm not waiting until morning."

Blue kept knocking until Cory thought his knuckles must hurt. She wondered how long he could keep going, but eventually Daisy's father came to the door.

"What are you doing?" he snapped as he turned on the fairy light next to the door. "Do you have any idea what time it is? This is a flower fairy household. We all have to get up bright and early."

"I apologize, sir, but this is a FLEA matter. I'm Officer Blue. I need to speak to your daughter, Daisy."

"She's in bed asleep and has been for hours," grumbled Daisy's father. "Can't this wait until morning?"

"I'm sorry, sir, but it can't. Please wake her for me."

"Is Daisy in some sort of trouble?"

"That depends on what she tells me," said Blue.

Daisy's father was grumbling when he walked off, but from the little Cory heard him say, she couldn't tell if he was mad at Blue or Daisy.

Blue turned to Cory, saying, "I hate to get people up like this, but sometimes it's unavoidable. Cory, do you . . . I didn't know you were hurt! How bad is it?"

"It's nothing," she assured him. "Just a few scrapes. I'm sure it looks bad because I haven't been able to get cleaned up yet."

"Cory! Blue! What are you doing here?" Daisy asked, rubbing the sleep from her eyes.

Her parents followed her to the doorway, looking as confused as Daisy. When they saw the blood on Cory's face, they all looked aghast.

"What happened to you?" Daisy asked.

"We were in an accident," said Cory.

Blue's jaw was set, his eyes angry when he said, "One that someone had planned, although it would have been a lot worse if it had gone the way they wanted it to. That's why we're here. Who did you tell that we were going to a party tonight?"

"What are you talking about?" Daisy asked, looking even more confused. "I didn't tell anyone anything!"

"You were the only person Cory told about the party at the pigs' house," said Blue. "You told someone. Was it a member of the Flower Fairy Guild?"

"No! I didn't tell them anything!" Daisy exclaimed. "The only one I might have mentioned it to is my new boyfriend, Tabbert. He wanted to meet you, and suggested we invite you out to dinner. I probably told him why you said you couldn't go when he asked again."

"Give me his full name," Blue said, taking an ink stick and a leaf out of his pocket.

"He's Tabbert Acklethwite," said Daisy. "I don't know if he has a middle name."

"You have a new boyfriend?" said her mother. "You didn't tell us!"

Blue took a small message pad from his pocket and began to write.

"How much do you have in there?" Cory asked.

Blue grunted and kept writing. "I have big pockets. All right," he said, looking up from the pad. "I just asked the FLEA officer on duty about Tabbert Acklethwite. We should hear back in a few minutes. Since this whole thing started, we've begun our own investigation of the guilds and its members." *Ping!* The pad gave off a faint chime. "Good. I have an answer already. It seems that Tabbert Acklethwite is a member of the Sandman Guild and is on unofficial leave."

"What does 'unofficial leave' mean?" asked Cory.

"That he's still a member, but not working as a sandman now," Blue told her.

"Which means he won't be working at night and can go out during the day," said Cory. "He can do things like date a flower fairy and question her about her friends."

"Or one friend in particular," Blue said. "When did you meet Tabbert, Daisy?"

"A few days ago," Daisy replied. "Are you saying that he asked me out so he could find out things about Cory?"

"It's possible," said Blue.

"I'm so sorry!" cried Daisy. "It never occurred to me that anyone would do that! What a no-good, lousy scumbag! Well, he's not getting anything more from me! I'm dumping him first thing tomorrow when I get home from work. Cory, you know I would never intentionally do anything to hurt you. You've been my best friend for as long as I can remember. No boyfriend is ever coming between us. I promise, this won't happen again!"

CHAPTER
7

When Cory stepped onto her porch the next morning, it looked as if half of the ogre solarcycle gang was waiting for her. There had to be at least thirty ogres, and they all waved when she started down the steps. She waved back and smiled, glad that they were there. Blue had assured her that some of them intended to stay at the courthouse, just in case. None of her ogre escorts had stayed when she testified in front of the big jury, and she'd almost been kidnapped. She felt safer already, knowing that they'd be in the building.

Cory and Blue wore their normal-looking helmets while the ogres wore their trademark troll-skull-shaped ones. When the gang started down the street, Cory and

Blue were in the middle, ensuring that no one could get close to them. People stopped and stared as the silent cavalcade rode past. Cory might have enjoyed the ride if she hadn't been so nervous about testifying.

When they reached the courthouse, the ogres who were staying parked their cycles in front of the building so everyone could see that they were there. As Blue walked Cory into the building, ogres surrounded them. The guards inside wouldn't let all the ogres go to the courtroom, but they did let Macks, Gnarl, Snifflit, and two others in. The rest would wait in the foyer and come running if they were needed.

Cory had to wait in another room until she was called. Blue went to talk to Natinia Blunk while two of the ogres stood outside the door and the others went into the courtroom to find seats. When it was time to go in, Officer Deeds came to fetch Cory. The moment she saw him, his image and that of her mother popped into her head. She grimaced at the thought.

"Nice to see you, too," grumbled the goblin officer. "I didn't think you'd show up. A lot of people don't like you right now."

"I'm aware of that," said Cory. "But I'm not here to get people to like me. I'm here to make sure the guilds can't get away with all the bad things they've been doing."

"We'll see," said the officer. "The guilds got themselves the best law upholder."

"No better than mine," Cory said, hoping it was true.

As Officer Deeds escorted her to the witness box, Cory looked around. The room was mostly filled with benches facing a raised platform. A lady elf dressed in a blue robe sat on the platform behind a big desk. There was a lower platform beside her with a single chair. Cory knew that was where the witnesses sat.

Although the sea of people turning to look at her made Cory nervous, seeing a few friendly faces helped calm her nerves. Blue was sitting in the back with Gnarl, Macks, and Snifflit. Lionel was seated closer to the front. Cory must have looked nervous because he gave her an encouraging smile and a wink. She saw Mary Mary, the head of the Tooth Fairy Guild, in the front row beside a violet-haired fairy woman who Cory recognized. Flora Petalsby was the head of the Flower Fairy Guild. She had done a lot of things to get attention for the guild over the years, and her picture was often in *The Fey Express*.

As Cory approached the witness chair, she glanced at the people seated at the side of the room. There were eleven people in the jury. Although she'd learned in school that humans preferred twelve jurors, the fey liked uneven numbers. Cory noticed that there were three fairies, two dwarves, and one ogre. The rest of the jurors were either nymphs or humans.

Cory was seated on the witness chair before she saw the defense law upholder. She was surprised to recognize him. It was Jasper Wilkins, the man she had matched with Mary Lambkin. Natinia Blunk was the first to approach her, however.

"How are you today, Miss Feathering? You look as if you've acquired some scrapes and bruises since I saw you last. Are you well enough to testify?"

Cory nodded. "Yes, I am."

"Then please tell the court exactly when the Tooth Fairy Guild began to harass you."

"It was shortly after I quit the guild. They weren't happy that I was leaving them and let me know it. First they sent messages, then they began to do things."

"Please tell us what they did," said Miss Blunk.

"I was staying with my uncle. They threw a large plaster tooth through the window."

"And did you call the FLEA about the window?"

"I did. Officer Deeds came out and I showed him the tooth."

"And then what happened?"

The eleven members of the jury listened intently while Cory told them about all the things the Tooth Fairy Guild had done. When she told them about the visits from members of the other guilds, the jury seemed even more interested. She described every nasty thing, including the rotting teeth and the hole in the ground the night before.

"Thank you, Miss Feathering," said Natinia when Cory was finished. "I may have more questions for you later."

Cory watched Jasper Wilkins approach the stand. He smiled and looked friendly, but she remembered what Natinia had told her about how he could be tricky.

"Good day, Miss Feathering," said Jasper. "Please tell the court why you quit the Tooth Fairy Guild."

"I wanted to do something that would help people," said Cory. "I didn't feel that I was really helping anyone by collecting teeth."

"I see," said Jasper. "So you're saying that your motives were altruistic. But isn't it true that you were not very good at your job? The last night you worked as a tooth fairy, you collected only four teeth. Wasn't money the real reason you quit?"

"I quit for a lot of reasons, but mainly because I wanted to help people," said Cory.

"So you thought your job as a tooth fairy was worthless," said Jasper.

"I didn't say that," Cory told him. "It just wasn't right for me."

"I see," said Jasper. "Just as a sandman wasn't right for you. Isn't it true that shortly after you quit your job with the Tooth Fairy Guild, you broke up with your boyfriend, a member of the Sandman Guild?"

"Yes, but—"

"And didn't you take on other jobs, working for people with no guild affiliations?"

"Yes, that's true, but—"

"Even your uncle, with whom you are now living, is not a guild member?"

"Yes," said Cory.

"Then it seems to me," Jasper said, turning to face the jury, "that Miss Feathering has hated guild members for some time now. She has done everything she can to damage their well-deserved good reputations."

"I've never accused them of doing anything that they didn't do!" Cory cried.

"Really? So you wouldn't use trickery to influence opinion?"

"Never!" said Cory.

"Tell me, Miss Feathering, have we ever met before?"

Cory shook her head. "No, we have not."

"Do you know my name?"

"Jasper Wilkins," said Cory.

"How did you learn my name?" asked Jasper.

"I asked around about you."

"But we never actually met before today?"

"No, we didn't." Cory was getting confused. She was sure the law upholder was trying to be tricky, but she had no idea where he was headed with his questions.

"Then why did you send me this message?" Jasper asked, and gestured to the court witch. The witch, a little lady in a floral dress with barrettes in her hair, waved her hand. An image of the message Cory had sent to Jasper appeared in the air above her.

Cory had a feeling that she knew where Jasper was headed and didn't like it one bit. "I thought you and Mary Lambkin would be right for each other," she replied.

"Without ever meeting me?" said Jasper. "Isn't it true that what you were really doing was trying to influence me in this trial? You had learned that I was going to be the DLU, and you wanted to bribe me to throw the trial your way!"

"That wasn't it at all! I didn't know you were involved in this case until you walked into the courtroom today!"

"We're supposed to believe that? Isn't your grandfather Lionel Feathering, who sits on the FLEA board?"

"Yes, but—"

"And isn't your current boyfriend FLEA officer-in-training Johnny Blue?"

"Yes," Cory admitted.

"And you want us to believe that no one, including your grandfather and your boyfriend, told you that I was on the case?"

"They didn't!"

"That's all I want to ask this witness for now. I'd like to call another witness. Mary Lambkin, would you please take the stand?"

When Cory left the stand, Mary Lambkin passed her, giving her a halfhearted smile. Mary took the seat on the low platform just as Cory sat down in a back row next to Blue.

"Please state your name," Jasper said to Mary.

"Mary Lambkin. Jasper, what is this about? You said I should meet you at court so we could go out for brunch."

"Ahem." Jasper cleared his throat. "We'll talk later. Are you the owner of Lambkin's Outerwear?"

"Yes," Mary replied.

"How do you know Cory Feathering?"

"I hired her as a matchmaker."

"Exactly how many matches has she made for you?"

Mary Lambkin smiled. "You were my first."

"Had you asked to meet me in particular?" asked Jasper.

"No, I'd never heard of you."

"So the first time you heard my name was when Cory Feathering arranged a date for us."

"That's true," said Mary.

"What happened on this date?"

Mary looked confused. "We had a good time? At least I did. You were a gentleman and we had a very nice dinner. I enjoyed our conversation and I thought you did, too."

Jasper cleared his throat again. "I did, but that's beside the point. So, were you hoping to see me again?"

"Yes, actually," Mary said, smiling shyly.

Jasper looked uncomfortable when he asked his next question. "Was it because you planned to trick me into telling you things about the trial that you could pass on to Cory Feathering?"

Mary gasped and a blush crept up her cheeks. "No, of course not! That's an awful thing to say!"

"So you're telling me that you weren't trying to make me fall in love with you so Cory Feathering would have leverage over me?" Jasper asked.

Mary was beet red by now and looked furious.

This is ridiculous, Cory thought. The only way she could defend herself and stop this line of questioning was to tell them about being a Cupid, but she wasn't about to do that. That left her with only one choice.

Bow! Cory thought as she got to her feet. Time stood still for everyone but Cory as the bow appeared in her hand and her quiver on her back. Plucking an arrow from her quiver, Cory read the name on its shaft. "Jasper Goodwell Wilkins" had appeared written in gold. Satisfied that she had the right one, Cory started to walk. Jasper was facing the stand, so Cory wanted to find an angle where she could hit his chest with her arrow. She was standing near Mary when she shot Jasper. The arrow hit him with a puff of sparkles.

Returning to the aisle by her seat, Cory took another arrow from her quiver. "Mary Patricia Lambkin" said the writing. When it hit Mary, the air around the couple sparkled with gold. Cory was back in her seat before the sparkles died away.

Suddenly, Mary and Jasper looked at each other as

if they had never seen the other person before. And then Mary was dashing from the witness box and Jasper was running to meet her. They were in each other's arms before most people knew what was happening.

"Order in the court!" the judge demanded, but Jasper and Mary were paying attention only to each other as they kissed in front of everyone.

"See, they were meant for each other," said the woman seated on the other side of Blue. Leaning forward to look past him, she said to Cory, "You *are* good! Can I hire you as my matchmaker?"

People around her laughed and Cory laughed with them. The only one who didn't was an elderly woman with silver hair who gave Cory a speculative look instead. When the woman finally turned away, she left Cory with the feeling that she disapproved.

Cory looked up when the crowd stirred; Jasper and Mary were running from the courtroom hand in hand. "Now what?" Cory whispered to Blue. He shrugged and turned toward the judge.

"Court is adjourned until one o'clock," the judge announced. "Let's see if we can find out what's going on with Wilkins!"

As the courtroom emptied into the hallway, Cory held tight to Blue's hand. When they left the room, the ogres clustered around them, moving to an empty space farther down the hall. They had been there only a few minutes when Lionel came to see her. "If you'll excuse me, gentlemen, I need to speak with my granddaughter alone," he told Cory's escorts.

He led Cory down the hall where no one could hear them. "I know why you did what you did, but you couldn't have picked a more public place," he told her. When she started to say something, he shook his head and said, "It's fine. I probably would have done the same thing. We don't always get to choose the time or place for the matches we make. Jasper Wilkins forced your hand. It wasn't an ideal situation, but I don't think there was anything else you could do. However, I just wanted you to know that there were a few people in that room who might have noticed the interruption in time. One in particular comes to mind, but I'll deal with her if I have to."

"Who was it?" asked Cory.

"A neighbor of mine," said Lionel. "Be that as it may, I just wanted to tell you that you may leave now. After Jasper's display, I doubt the defense is going to follow that line of questioning any further. They have other witnesses lined up for today. If they need you again in the future, they'll let you know."

"Thank you, Grandfather. Other than today, how is the trial going?" Cory asked him.

Lionel shrugged. "Some days are better than others. Right now it could go either way. Take care, my dear. Keep your bodyguards until the trial is over. It's only just begun."

CHAPTER

8

Cory wasn't happy about the way things had gone at court, but she was sure it could have been worse. She was glad it was over, at least for now, and hoped she wouldn't be called back.

After the ogres escorted Cory and Blue home, Macks declared that he was going to get the yard ready for some shrubs Micah planned to buy. Blue was walking around the yard with him when Cory went inside to change her clothes and make lunch. She had just gotten out a loaf of bread when Blue came to the door.

"Your mother is here to see you," he said. "Do you want me to send her away or stay while you talk to her?"

Cory sighed. One of the last people she wanted to see right then was her mother. "I'll talk to her in the main room," she said, setting down the bread. "Although I really don't want to hear what she has to say."

"All right," said Blue, "but I'll be right outside if you need me."

When Blue opened the door, Delphinium came bustling in. Before her mother could speak, Cory had a flash of the images of Delphinium and Officer Deeds. She forced the images away by focusing on what her mother was saying.

"You went through with it! I didn't think you really would. I hope you're satisfied. You're trying to take down one of the great institutions of the fey world."

Cory sighed. "I'm not trying to take anything down, Mother. I just did what I thought was right. The guilds have been getting away with too much for too long."

"That guild put food on our table while you were growing up. They've been good to us, and you turned them in to the law! I am so disappointed in you. I thought I'd raised you better than this."

"And I think you should be happy that I'm able to stand up for myself," said Cory. "You care more about your precious guild than you do about me. You don't care that they're actively trying to hurt me now and have been for some time."

"I warned you about that," said Delphinium. "It's your own fault that you didn't listen."

"Why did you come over, Mother? You've already disowned me. You said I would never see you again. Giving up on your promise already?"

"I came to tell you that it isn't too late. You can still recant your testimony. Tell them that you were mistaken. The people in the guilds aren't the horrible monsters you're making them out to be!"

"I'm not recanting anything, except my decision to talk to you. Good-bye, Mother."

When Delphinium made no effort to leave, Cory opened the door. "Blue, my mother is leaving now. She just won't admit it."

"Do you need some help, Mrs. Feathering?" Blue said as he stepped inside.

With a last scornful look at Cory, her mother strode from the room, her head held high.

"That was awful," Cory told Blue as he shut the door. "Next time I say that I'll talk to her, don't listen to me. Now on to something really important. How many sandwiches do you and Macks want?"

Blue was helping Cory clean up the kitchen after lunch when she received a message.

Dear Cory,

My mother is in town, and we thought it would be nice to have dinner with you and Blue. If you are able to come, I'll pick you up outside your house at six o'clock this evening.

Your friend,
Jack B. Nimble

"That would be fun," said Cory. "I'd love to see them."

"Then tell them that we'll be ready by six," said Blue. "I don't think we'll need to take a bodyguard with us. Jack is just as conscious of security as we are."

Cory spent the rest of the afternoon cleaning the bathing room, sweeping the floors, and doing laundry while Blue and Macks worked outside. When it was time to get ready, Macks read a book while Cory and Blue changed their clothes. Remembering the last time Jack Nimble gave her a ride, she put on slacks and a pale pink sweater, then grabbed a light jacket.

Cory and Blue were standing in the front yard when Jack's hot-air balloon landed in the street. Macks was waiting with them, but as soon as they climbed into the basket under the balloon, he waved good-bye and rode away on his solar cycle. Although Cory had ridden in the basket once before, she still found it fascinating. She loved watching Jack control the height of their flight by heating or releasing hot air.

Blue didn't seem to enjoy it nearly as much as Cory did. When she glanced at him to tell him something about one of the buildings below, his face was pale and his mouth looked pinched. "Are you all right?" she asked.

Blue closed his eyes. "I'll be fine once we land."

"Have you ever flown before?" Jack asked him.

"No. I had no idea it would be like this," Blue said, and swallowed hard.

"I think he's airsick," Cory whispered to Jack.

"Some people can't handle flying," Jack whispered back. "I'd heard that a lot of ogres get really sick, but Blue is only half ogre. I thought he'd be fine."

"Please stop talking about it," Blue told them. "That only makes it worse. Are we almost there?"

"Where are we going anyway?" Cory asked Jack.

"My house," he told her. "My mother and Marjorie are making supper together. It isn't far now. I live on the north side of town. If you look past that park and that big building on the left, you can just make out my roof."

"Your house is big enough to see from here?" Cory exclaimed.

"Nimble Sports is doing very well," Jack said with a grin.

They landed on the front lawn of one of the bigger houses in the area. A tall fence surrounded the lawn on every side. Once they were on the ground, all they could see beyond the fence were the roofs of the neighboring houses.

"Wow!" said Cory. "Your house is as big as my grandfather's."

"I've invited my mother to come live here, but she prefers the country. The trouble with the guilds might change her mind, though. I think she's lonely where she lives now. Go on in while I secure the balloon. You'll find Marjorie and my mother in the kitchen."

"Mind if I stay with you?" Blue asked Jack. "I need to sit still for a while."

"The fresh air might help, too," Cory said, and gave him a kiss on the cheek. "I'll see you inside."

"Go in the back door on your left," Jack told her. "The kitchen is just down the hall."

Although Cory was reluctant to leave Blue, she didn't think there was anything she could do to help him. Following Jack's directions, she went inside and started looking for the kitchen. It was a huge, new house and she could easily have gotten lost if she hadn't heard Marjorie and Stella laughing.

"Good evening, ladies," Cory said as she walked into the kitchen.

"Cory!" Stella said. Dropping a dish towel on the table, she hurried over to give Cory a hug. "I heard you had your ordeal today. So did I, right before you.

Jack hustled me out of there afterward or I would have seen you."

"How did it go?" asked Cory.

"It was absolutely dreadful," Stella said, making a disgusted face. "That Jasper Wilkins is such a troll! I didn't know that humans could be that nasty. He made me look like an idiot and a liar. I couldn't wait to get out of there."

"I don't mean to interrupt," said Marjorie, "but where's Blue?"

"He'll be in soon," Cory told them. "He got really airsick on his way here."

"Oh, dear!" said Marjorie. "I should have thought of that! Most ogres can't handle flying. I did some research for a book once and learned a lot about them. Blue is only half ogre, though, isn't he?"

Cory nodded. "I'm still not sure if he's more like an ogre or a human. I guess I'm learning more about him every day."

Jack took a deep breath as he came into the room. "Something smells really good. What's for supper?"

"I cooked roast beef. I know how much ogres like meat," said Marjorie. "And your mother steamed some fish for those who don't eat meat."

"Perfect!" Jack said, giving her a kiss. "How long before everything is ready?"

"It's ready now. We can eat as soon as you wash up," his mother told him.

Blue came into the room then, looking a little less pale. He gave Cory a wan smile and took a seat on a stool in the corner.

"I have just the thing for an upset stomach," said Stella, and began to bustle around the kitchen, finding the necessary ingredients. When she had it ready, she handed a cup to Blue. "Drink all of it and you'll feel fine in a few minutes."

Blue looked skeptical. After sniffing the drink and taking a tentative taste, he chugged the entire contents of the cup. "That wasn't bad," he told her. "Thanks!"

Cory helped Stella and Marjorie take the food to the table. By the time they were ready, Blue was looking normal again.

After everyone was seated and had helped themselves from heaping platters, Jack said, "I have an announcement. Mother, I'm sure you already guessed, but we didn't want to make it official until after you'd already testified and could relax. Marjorie and I are getting married."

"That's wonderful news!" exclaimed Cory.

"I knew it!" said Stella. "It's about time. The way you two look at each other, I knew you'd pop the question soon. Have you talked about children yet?"

"Mother, give us time!" Jack said, laughing.

"Actually, we have talked about it," said Marjorie. "And we both want lots of children."

"Good!" Stella cried. "That's just what I wanted to hear."

Cory glanced at Blue. He was gazing at her with a wistful look in his eyes, making her wonder exactly what he was thinking.

"No one's eating my green beans!" said Stella. "Eat up. There's a lot more in the kitchen."

Everyone started eating then. The food was delicious and plentiful. Cory noticed that Blue really enjoyed the roast beef. She'd had no idea he liked meat so much.

"I'm reading a really good book," Jack told them when Marjorie left the table to get dessert. "I bought it from a man who imports them through secret channels from the human world. He has a stand at the Black Market. You know where that is, don't you? It's across the street from the Green Market."

"What kind of book is it?" asked Blue.

"It's a western. I don't know if you're familiar with them, but—"

Blue's eyes lit up. "I love westerns, but they're so hard to find!"

"I have some I can give you," said Jack. "I've already read them at least three times each."

"That would be great!" said Blue.

"Here it is! I made a chocolate, chocolate-chip pie!" said Marjorie, setting it on the table. "I know that ogres are notorious for having a sweet tooth. Blue, let me give you a big piece."

Cory was surprised when he ate two huge pieces. He loved the berry pies she made at home, but she'd never thought about him having a sweet tooth.

Thinking about all the things she didn't know about Blue, Cory only half listened as Marjorie described the new book she was writing, and Stella told her about her new hobby, embroidery. When it was time to leave, Cory turned to Jack. "I love that you gave us a ride in your hot-air balloon, but I don't think we should go home that way, considering how sick it made Blue. I think we should take the pedal-bus instead."

"I wouldn't think of it!" said Jack. "I agree that you shouldn't fly, but there's no need to take the pedal-bus. You can borrow my solar cycle. I have one of those new batteries in it. You won't even have to pedal to get it started."

"That's awfully kind of you, but—" Cory began.

"I'll come by tomorrow to pick it up," said Jack.

"We're just glad you could come for supper," said Marjorie. "We don't have friends over very often, because so many people are angry that Stella is testifying against the guilds. Right now, we're not even sure who we can trust, other than you two."

"We know how you feel," Cory said, thinking of Daisy.

They were riding home on Jack's solar cycle when Blue glanced over his shoulder at Cory. "Thanks for suggesting something other than a balloon ride home. I don't know if I could have handled it again."

"You're very welcome," Cory told him, happy that she'd finally done something for him.

CHAPTER
9

Cory was reading *The Fey Express* at breakfast the next morning when she saw an article about Goldilocks and Prince Rupert. "This says that Princess Goldilocks and Prince Rupert are in town. It's so odd seeing Goldilocks referred to as 'Princess.' It doesn't mention where they're staying, but I bet it's with her mother. I wonder what Rupert thinks of the shoe house and all the children."

Gladys Piper lived in a shoe-shaped house with all of her youngest children. Cory was familiar with the house and the large family, having babysat the younger children before she met Goldilocks.

"I still have to give Goldilocks her necklace," said Cory. "It was one of the things I retrieved from the highwaymen who stole our jewelry. I know the necklace was important to Goldilocks, but I wasn't sure how to get it to her safely before this. I'll send a message to her mother and ask if I can bring it over today."

"She might be a little busy with royalty in the house," said Blue.

"I just want to drop it off," Cory replied.

Ping! A message had arrived in the basket. Cory retrieved it and brought it back to the table. "Can you believe it? This is from Gladys. She says that she has company who would love to see me. She wants to know if I can come over today."

"That's awfully nice of her," said Micah. "I didn't know that Goldilocks thought you were such a good friend."

"I didn't, either," said Cory. "Zephyr is rehearsing tonight, so I have to eat an early dinner. I could go see Goldilocks this morning. Macks and I can head over there as soon as he gets here. I'll put my hair up and wear my dark glasses again. That seemed to work well last time."

When Cory told Macks that they were going to the shoe house on North Shore Road, he knew exactly where it was located. "I've fished in Wander Lake many times," he told her. "The best way to get to the lake is to go down North Shore Road. Every time I go past that house, I wish I could see inside."

"Then you're in luck," said Cory. "Because it looks as if you'll get your chance today."

It didn't take them long to reach North Shore Road, but the FLEA had blocked it and weren't letting anyone past. Curious neighbors were clustered near the roadblock, trying to see what was going on.

"Sorry, sir," one of the officers told Macks. "The road is closed for the day."

"But I was invited," Cory told the officer. "Gladys Piper sent me a message this morning."

"Let me see if you're on the list. What is your name, miss?"

"Cory Feathering," she said softly, not wanting to let all the neighbors know.

"I'm sorry, I didn't catch that. You'll have to speak up."

"Cory Feathering," she said in a louder voice.

Cory tried not to look when there was a stir among the neighbors. Apparently, they had heard her. So had the FLEA officer. He gave her an appraising glance before turning back to the leaf he held in his hand.

"Yes, you're on the list. You may go through."

The FLEA officer moved the blockade enough to let Macks's solar cycle through. Even then they weren't able to drive all the way to the shoe house. Another FLEA officer stopped them when they were two houses away. "You'll have to park your cycle here, sir," the officer said, pointing to a spot by the side of the road.

After parking the cycle, they walked up to the front door of the shoe house without anyone else stopping them. While Cory knocked on the door, Macks ogled the house like a tourist, craning his neck to see the laces dangling high above. Gladys answered the door a moment later. "Oh, good, you're here. And you've brought your boyfriend."

"This is Macks," said Cory. "He's not my boyfriend."

"I'm her bodyguard," said Macks.

"Really!" said Gladys. "I've seen the posters and heard about the court case, but I didn't know you needed a bodyguard. Well, come on in. Goldilocks and Serelia are in the kitchen. Rupert has taken the children shopping. We were just about to have a cup of tea. Would you like some?"

"Serelia is here?" said Cory.

Gladys nodded. "She traveled with Goldilocks and Rupert. Ah, here we are. Sit wherever you'd like. There are plenty of chairs!"

Gladys's husband, the Pied Piper, had kidnapped forty-two children and brought them to the fey world. After he was convicted of kidnapping, he'd been sent to prison, leaving Gladys to raise the children on her own. With such a big family, the house was crammed with furniture, leaving very little room to move around.

"Hi!" Goldilocks said in a cheerful voice as Cory took a seat.

"Hi!" Cory said to Goldilocks and Serelia. She was about to introduce Macks to them when she noticed that he was standing by the door, looking confused. "Oh, right. You're too big to fit in any of the chairs. Would you like to wait outside instead?"

Macks nodded, looking grateful. "I'll be by the front door if you need me," he said before hurrying out.

"So you're married now," Cory said to Goldilocks. "That's wonderful! How do you like living in the castle?"

"It's a lot bigger than I'm used to. I got lost three times the day you left," said Goldilocks.

Cory turned to Serelia. The woman was one of the most powerful water nymphs around and took care of all the water issues at Misty Falls, Prince Rupert's ancestral home. "And you came with Goldilocks and Rupert?" Cory asked her.

Serelia nodded. "I came to meet Rina. I was hoping you could arrange it for today. We aren't going to be here long."

Goldilocks set her teacup down with a loud *clink*. "We really just came to get Mother and the children. I want them to come live in the castle. There's so much room there, and Rupert said that we can get tutors for the children."

"We're going, but I told Goldilocks that I don't know if we'll stay there for good," said Gladys. "I don't want to impose on her in-laws."

"It was Rupert's idea," Goldilocks said. "I'm sure his mother will get used to it."

"I thought you said his parents liked the idea," said Gladys. "I'm not going if they don't want us there."

"I'm sure they'll love you, Mother," Goldilocks told her. "They'll love the children, too. I'm just not sure what to do about Tom Tom."

The only child Gladys had given birth to was Tom Tom. He was an employee of the Tooth Fairy Guild and one of the people who had tormented Cory.

"Doesn't he have to stay around until his trial?" asked Cory. After all the nasty things he had done to Cory, Tom Tom had been arrested. The Tooth Fairy Guild had posted bail for him, getting him out of jail.

"That's just it," said Goldilocks. "He has to stay in town. He's been living here with Mother, but if she moves away and sells the house, where is he going to go?"

"That boy has been in trouble his entire life," said Gladys. "I've tried to keep him in line, but he doesn't listen to anyone. I really don't know if this is a good time for me to leave."

"But Mother . . . ," Goldilocks began.

"I should probably go see if Rina is home," said Cory. She pushed her chair back and stood, but Goldilocks and Gladys were too busy arguing to notice. Taking the cloth bag holding the necklace from her purse, Cory slid it across the table to Goldilocks. The girl barely glanced at Cory, but she did begin to fiddle with the bag. When mother and daughter continued to argue, Cory glanced at Serelia and they left the room together.

Macks was sitting on the grass, waiting for Cory when she stepped outside. "We have to go down the street," she told him. "I need to find out if Rina is home so I can introduce her to Serelia. Serelia, this is Macks. He's my bodyguard while the trial is going on."

"It's nice to meet you, Macks," said Serelia. "I've heard about that trial! What a mess. I don't get involved in guild politics anymore, which is just the way I like it. From what I've heard, though, I think you're doing the right thing. I know I wouldn't take kindly to a guild interfering in my personal life."

"Where does this Rina person live?" asked Macks. "I can go on ahead and see if she's home."

"Rina is a child. She lives with her parents in the house at the end of the street," said Cory. "Their house is right next to the lake."

"I'll go find out," Macks told her, and headed off.

Cory and Serelia started walking in that direction, talking as they went. "When did you get here?" Cory asked.

"Yesterday," said Serelia. "I rode in the coach with Goldilocks and Rupert. Longest trip of my life. Those two couldn't do anything but make eyes at each other when they weren't kissing. When I wasn't taking a nap, I pretended to be just so I wouldn't have to see them. That's Rina's house, huh? A house right next to a lake is perfect for a water nymph."

"I understand Rina's mother has a hard time keeping her out of the water," said Cory.

"Sounds like me when I was a girl," said Serelia. "Look, your bodyguard is coming back."

Macks looked embarrassed when he reached them. "They're home," he said. "At least I assume it's them. A woman and a little girl were in the yard when I walked up. They took one look at me, ran in the house, and locked the door. You might want to go to the door while I stay here by the street. Some people are really scared of ogres."

"I hadn't thought of that," said Cory. "I'm so used to you and your friends that I don't think of you as anything but people. Thank you for checking on them for me, Macks. I'm sorry they were so rude."

"Not rude so much as scared," said Macks. "You can't fault a person for that."

Cory and Serelia walked to the front door together. When Cory knocked, no one came to the door until she called, "It's me, Cory! I've brought Serelia Quirt to meet you."

Rina's mother must have been standing just inside because the door opened right away. "Cory!" cried Minerva. "You shouldn't be out there. There's an ogre lurking around the neighborhood!"

"Actually, Macks is a friend of mine. He walked ahead to see if you were home," said Cory. "I brought Serelia Quirt to meet you and Rina."

Minerva's eyes opened wide when she turned to Serelia. "Miss Quirt! What an honor! Thank you so much for coming!"

"I'll leave you now so you can talk," Cory said. "Have a good trip back, Serelia. It was nice to see you again."

"And you, Cory," said Serelia. "Thanks for your help."

"Do people react to you like that very often?" Cory asked Macks as they returned to his solar cycle.

"Not too often," he replied. "It's mostly people who aren't used to seeing ogres. We don't have a good reputation. People who don't know us are the ones who tend to believe it."

"People who don't know the truth can believe the strangest things," said Cory.

They were riding the solar cycle toward the road-block when Cory glanced back at the shoe house. She wondered what was going to happen to it if the family moved away. It was perfect for a family with so many children, but she couldn't imagine who else might want to live there.

The FLEA officer had already opened the barricade for them when they reached it, so they drove past without stopping. Cory was about to say something to Macks when the first clod of dirt hit her helmet.

"Put your head down!" Macks shouted as they were pelted with more clods of dirt.

Cory ducked, but that didn't stop her from seeing the flower fairies standing by the edge of the road, throwing dirt at them. *So much for my disguise*, she thought as she and Macks sped away on the solar cycle.

⫸➤

Micah was home from work earlier than usual that night, so he was there to eat an early supper with Cory and Blue. On their way to Olot's cave, Cory peeked over Blue's shoulder, watching out for any more holes. When they reached the cave without incident, Cory was happy to get inside. Daisy was already there, and she came running over when Cory walked in.

"I dumped Tabbert," she told Cory. "Guess what I did last night?"

"Found a new boyfriend?" said Cory.

"No, silly! I started writing a song. It's about friendship. Don't you get it? I'm writing a song about you and me. When it's done, I'll bring it to rehearsal and we can try it out. It's really good, so far."

"That's wonderful," Cory said, giving her friend a hug. "I'm sorry Tabbert was such a lousy boyfriend."

Daisy shrugged. "Boyfriends come and go, but a best friend is forever!"

"Everyone!" Olot announced. "I'd like you to meet Dillert. He's going to take over Goldilocks's old job."

"Hello, everyone," said Dillert, flashing a grin that showed off his perfect white teeth. The pointy ears peeking through his dark curls identified him as a fairy, although he was taller than most and broader across the shoulders.

"I think I dumped Tabbert just in time," Daisy whispered to Cory. "Do you see this guy? Hello, Mr. Right!"

Cory laughed and shook her head. "You'll never give up, will you Daisy?"

"Why should I?" Daisy said as she started toward the place she usually stood. "I'll find the right one someday."

Cory stood motionless as an image of Daisy formed in her mind. She waited for another image to appear, willing it to happen, but none did. *It will someday*, Cory thought. She was sure of it.

The rehearsal went longer than usual when Olot insisted that they practice a song they'd long found troublesome. They had it almost perfect when they finally quit for the night.

Cory was gathering up her possessions, getting ready to leave, when Olot called out, "Don't forget, we have a gig tomorrow. We're playing at my cousin Itchy Butt's birthday party. He says there will be plenty of food, so come hungry and ready to play!"

"Another ogre party," Cory said to Blue as they walked out the door. "Whatever happens, I am not taking part in any three-legged races!"

Cory and Blue were both tired when they reached Micah's house that night. Cory's uncle was already in bed asleep, so Cory said good night to Blue and left to get ready for bed. Weegie and Noodles were both curled up in Noodles's bed, snoring gently. Wondering why the woodchucks were sleeping inside, Cory brushed her teeth and changed into her nightgown. Blue was asleep on the main room floor before Cory turned out her lights, and it wasn't long before she was asleep as well.

A few hours later, Cory woke to Weegie's shriek. "Ow! That hurt, you big dummy. Why are you walking around like that at night? You're not Blue! Who are you?"

Cory shot out of bed and into the main room, nearly running into Micah as he appeared in his doorway. Weegie was there, glaring at a stooped figure struggling in Blue's grip. The indistinct figure was nearly as big as Blue, but as Micah walked around the room, lighting fairy lights, it seemed to shrink until it was no bigger than a ten-year-old boy.

"Well, I'll be!" Micah said as he examined the figure. "I know what you are! You're a Worry That Won't Let You Sleep at Night! I've read about you in the old books, but I wasn't sure you really existed."

The creature moaned, covering its face with its hand. Cory began to worry that it was in pain.

"I guess we were due for another monster," said Blue. "All right, Worry That . . . whatever you're called, I'll need your name and guild affiliation to start with."

When the monster hunched into itself and refused to speak, Blue gave him a shake. "I don't have all night for this. Speak up!"

"I know what to do," said Micah, and he ran from the room.

"My back hurts!" Weegie said, glowering at the creature. "I heard a sound and came out to look around, and that stupid monster stepped on me!"

Noodles bumped her head with his and began to lick her. They were nuzzling each other when Micah returned, bringing a big tube with a button on the side. Aiming the tube at the monster, he pressed the button and a bright light shot out like a ray from a miniature sun.

The monster cowered and began to whimper, rubbing its eyes with its knuckles.

"Worry monsters are a lot less threatening once you examine them in daylight," said Micah.

The creature looked up to reveal big eyes with deep

purple circles underneath. Its shoulders slumped as it dragged its feet backward, away from Micah's light.

"Tell me your name and guild affiliation," Blue ordered. He stepped closer so that he towered over the creature, and gave it another shake.

"My name is Sidney Glomer," it said in a mournful voice. "I'm a member of the Itinerant Troublemakers Guild."

"Do you suppose this is one of the Big Baddies that the ITG was going to send?" asked Cory.

"I don't know," said Micah. "I don't know that much about them."

After Sidney answered the rest of Blue's questions, Blue walked him to the door and let him go. The creature shuffled off, making little moaning sounds.

"I hope we can get some sleep now," said Micah. "We have to get up in a few hours."

Cory nodded and they all went back to bed. Although she was exhausted, she couldn't stop thinking about the monster. It had looked so sad and pitiful that she felt sorry for it. She began to worry that it might be sick. Then she began to worry about the other monsters that the ITG might send their way. What exactly was a Big Baddie? Was each monster going to be worse than the last? It looked like the trial might not ever end. Would the ITG send monsters to plague them the entire time? And what if the guilds won the case? Would she have to leave town to avoid their constant persecution?

Cory eventually fell asleep again, but only because she was exhausted. It was a restless sleep, however, filled with troubling dreams.

CHAPTER
10

*C*ory was dreaming about her mother and Officer Deeds when she forced herself to wake up the next morning. "That's one match I'm not going to make," she told herself as she climbed out of bed. She was almost as tired as when she'd gone to bed the night before and thought wistfully about taking a nap later. "I know there's something we have to do today," she muttered as she looked for the clothes she planned to wear. "I just can't remember what it is."

Dressed and ready to go out, Cory left her room a little later than usual. When she passed through the main room on the way to the kitchen, she saw that Blue's makeshift bed had already been put away. She found Blue in the kitchen, talking to Micah. It looked as if they had both been up for a while; they were dressed and had nearly finished eating their breakfast.

"Where did you get that light you used on the monster last night?" Blue was asking Micah.

"My mother gave it to me for my birthday a few years ago. I've noticed that when people don't know what to give me, I often get fairy tube lights. I have a drawer full of them in my bedroom."

"That was a good, strong light," said Blue. "I'll have to get one of those. Oh, good, Cory's up. Hey, sleepyhead. How are you today?"

"I feel like something a woodchuck dragged in. Speaking of woodchucks, how are Noodles and Weegie?"

"Noodles is fine, but Weegie is still complaining about her back. I let them out when I got up," said Micah. "Poor Weegie wanted to sleep inside last night because she wasn't feeling well, and now this."

"Did you want some breakfast?" Blue asked.

Cory shook her head. "I think I'll go visit my grandfather Lionel today. I want to talk to him about something. If I go in the morning, he always gives me breakfast. I think the putti would be disappointed if they couldn't feed me."

"If you're not going to sit down, I won't dawdle any longer," Micah said as he stood. "I woke up worried that

I'd be late for work, so I want to head in a little early. Have a good day, you two."

"We will," said Blue. "I should get going as well. Macks should be here soon. Today is Itchy Butt's birthday party and I requested guard duty. After what happened at the last ogre party, the captain agrees that I should go. Now I'm worried that two guards might not be enough. Maybe I should request more backup."

"That's what I forgot!" said Cory. "I knew there was something we were supposed to do. It's Itchy Butt's party!"

There was a knock at the front door and Blue pushed his seat back. "I'll see you in a few hours," he said, and gave Cory a quick kiss. "I need to take care of some leaf work at the station before we go to the party."

Blue was on the porch talking to Macks when Cory heard the *ping!* of a message arriving in the basket. While Cory was on her way to get it, another message arrived. The first one was from Serelia.

Cory,
 We're heading back to Misty Falls today. Rina is going with us. She shows a lot of promise. Thank you for introducing us. I think she's going to be the assistant I've always wanted and

*eventually the replacement I need. Let me know
if there's ever anything I can do for you.*

Serelia Quirt

"Good," Cory murmured. Rina was finally going to get the training she deserved.

The second note was from Rina's mother.

*Cory,
     Thank you so much for telling us about
Serelia. Rina is leaving with her today to
begin her studies. Everything has turned out
so well because of you. Thanks!*

Minerva Diver

"I'm glad they're happy," said Cory.

Macks was waiting for her on the porch when she went outside. "Blue said you wanted to go somewhere this morning," said the ogre.

Cory nodded as she started down the steps. "You and I are going to see my grandfather Lionel. Have you ever met any putti?"

"Any whatti?" he asked.

"You'll see soon enough," Cory said with a laugh.

Cory smiled at Macks's expression when they arrived at

Lionel's home. His eyes were wide and his mouth hung open, making him look even scarier than usual. "Your grandfather lives here?" he asked as his gaze traveled over the vast lawn, heart-shaped driveway, and huge house.

"He does," Cory said, leading the way up the drive. "But he doesn't live alone."

Macks hung back as Cory climbed the steps and pressed the heart-shaped doorbell. "I don't think I should go in," he said from the bottom of the steps. "Everything looks very grand. If I go in, I might break something."

Cory smiled and gestured to him. "You'll be fine. I'm sure the putti will watch out for you."

"You never told me what putti are," said Macks as he climbed the steps with reluctance.

"You'll know in just a minute," said Cory. "Orville is a putti."

Macks reached up to scratch his head. "Who is Orville?"

The door opened and a little man who looked like a bald-headed baby dressed in slacks and a shirt stood there. He grinned when he saw Cory, but his eyebrows shot up when he noticed Macks.

"Orville, I'd like you to meet my friend, Macks. Macks, this is my friend, Orville."

The putti's smile grew broader when he heard Cory call him her friend. He extended his hand to Macks, saying, "It's nice to meet you" in a surprisingly deep voice.

Macks had to bend down to shake Orville's hand. When he did, the putti's smooth babylike hand disappeared in the ogre's huge, rough-skinned one. "It's nice to meet you, too," said Macks. "I'm actually Cory's bodyguard."

"Very good," said Orville before he turned to Cory. "Your grandfather just started his breakfast," he said, and began to lead the way.

When Cory glanced at Macks, he looked awestruck as he took everything in. They were walking down a long, marble-floored corridor when Orville opened a door and said to Macks, "You may wait in here. I'll tell Creampuff that you're hungry."

"How did you know that?" asked Macks.

Orville shrugged. "Ogres always are."

The putti disappeared into the room. When he came out, he waved Macks in and shut the door behind him. "I assume that you may want to discuss things with your grandfather that you do not want to share with your bodyguard," said Orville. "We'll take care of him until you're ready to go."

"Thank you," Cory told him. "I doubt I'll be staying long."

"Long enough for breakfast, I hope?" the putti asked her.

"Of course!" she said, and her smile was rewarded with one of his.

Her grandfather was seated on the stone terrace at the back of the house, just as he always was in the morning. He looked up as she walked through the door. "My dear! It's good to see you. Please join me."

Cory took her usual seat across from Lionel. "I have a question for you. I've been having the same vision, but it's for a match I do *not* want to make. I've tried to ignore it, but the same vision keeps coming back. My question is, if I don't make this particular match, will this vision eventually stop?"

"May I ask who is in this vision?" said Lionel.

Cory made a face as if she tasted something sour. "It's my mother and the goblin FLEA officer, Deeds."

Uncontrollable laughter exploded from Lionel until his eyes watered and he was holding his sides. It was not the reaction Cory had expected. He grew calmer and wiped his eyes when Orville emerged from the house carrying a tray laden with dishes. No one spoke while Orville set the glass of cider and plates of eggs, fried cod, fruit salad, and spiced grains on the table. It wasn't until the putti had shut the door that Cory said, "I'm glad you think it's so funny."

"I must apologize," her grandfather said, stifling a chuckle, "but I've known Delphinium for years and never *saw* her in a vision with anyone. And for her to finally be in a vision with a goblin no less . . . I think it's the funniest thing I've ever heard!"

Cory's lips twitched into a smile. "It is pretty funny when you think about it. But that still leaves me with the question of what will happen if I don't match them."

"I don't know," said her grandfather. "To be honest, I've never had a match that I refused to make, but then I've never had one I didn't like that was so close to home. All I can say is that you should trust in yourself. I'm sure you'll do the right thing, although it may not be the easiest. Aside from your vision, how are things going?"

Cory took a sip of her cider before answering. "Not well, I'm afraid. I can't go anywhere without seeing posters denouncing me. I try to disguise myself when I go out in public, but it doesn't always work. On the way home from the pigs' party, tooth fairies dumped rotting teeth on Blue and me. When we were going down the mountain, someone had dug a hole in the road that we narrowly avoided with the solar cycle."

"I heard about that when you testified in court," said Lionel. "I think flower fairies probably dug it. They're the experts on digging holes."

"That's what we thought, too," said Cory. "And then just last night we had a visit from a member of the Itinerant Troublemakers Guild. Micah said he was a Worry That Won't Let You Sleep at Night."

Lionel looked surprised. "Really? And how do you feel now?"

"Fine," Cory said with a shrug.

"No new worries or concerns?"

"Now that you mention it, I had a terrible time going back to sleep after Blue kicked the monster out," said Cory. "I kept worrying about, well, everything! And this morning Micah said he was worried about being late to work, and Blue was worried about the security for a party this afternoon."

Lionel nodded. "That's what a Worry That Won't Let You Sleep at Night does. He doesn't look frightening, but he is very powerful."

"But he didn't *do* anything," said Cory.

"All he had to do was get into your house. He radiates worry like Cupids can radiate love. And that's your solution right there."

"What do you mean about radiating love?" asked Cory. "I don't do that."

"You can if you try," her grandfather told her. "To get rid of the worry in your house, wait until it's dark out, turn out all the lights in the room, spread your wings, and think about love. You'll be using your true strength to banish the bad feelings that the Worry creature brought into your home."

"Have you ever done it?" Cory asked.

"I've done it for any negative feelings that have been brought into the house," he replied. "And it works every time."

Cory didn't see Macks again until she was leaving. The ogre looked happy and satisfied when Orville retrieved him from the kitchen. "What did you do all morning?" Cory asked as they headed toward the solar cycle.

"I ate," Macks said, smacking his lips. "That little putti chef, Creampuff, is one good cook! We can go back there any time you want!"

Cory laughed. "I'll keep that in mind."

When they reached Micah's house, Blue was there along with two other ogres. "These two gentleogres are my backup," he said, gesturing to the ogres who were wrestling a new tree into one of the holes they'd dug. "The one with the green hair is Twark. The one with three hairs on his head is Skweely. They're both old friends of mine. I asked them to go to the party with us for added security. We decided to work on the yard until it was time to go."

"When you said you thought you might need more backup, I thought you meant more FLEA officers," said Cory.

"Why would I ask them?" said Blue. "Ogres are much better at handling anything bad that comes along."

"Except ice," said Cory.

"Well, that's true," Blue said with a rueful smile. "But I doubt very much the guilds will try that again. So, now that you're here, why don't you tell me where you want these shrubs? Micah bought them the other day. I told him that I would plant them. They were delivered this morning right after I got back."

"Didn't Micah tell you where he wanted everything planted?" Cory asked.

Blue shook his head. "Just the one tree. He said that the rest would be up to you. So, where do you want them?"

Cory and Blue walked around, trying to decide where to plant everything, while Macks helped the other ogres plant the tree. Noodles chewed a stick beside Weegie, who was making comments about how woodchucks dug better holes. When the ogres started laughing at her, she stalked off, insulted.

"How is the trial going?" Cory asked after they'd decided where to plant the last shrub.

"There's not much I can tell you, other than that Miss Blunk has found other abused fairies to testify. The guilds have been making the members who quit miserable for years. But even with the new testimony, the guilds are—"

Cory and Blue both looked up when a whooshing sound emerged from the forested park across the street. Something large and long was hurtling toward them. It wasn't until it hit the sidewalk with a splintering crash that Cory saw it was an entire tree, roots and all. The three ogres became alert. Apparently, this was the kind of thing they understood. They had started toward Cory and Blue when a huge brown shape shot from the forest with an earsplitting roar. The ground shook as it thundered across the road, wielding another tree.

"What is that?" cried Cory as the three ogres jumped in front of her and Blue.

"That, my sweet, is a Bigfoot," said Blue. "We learned about them in one of my FLEA classes. I'm glad I asked Skweely and Twark to go to the party with us. Either Macks or I might have been a match for a Bigfoot, but he doesn't stand a chance against the four of us."

"He seems pretty handy with that tree trunk," Cory said as the Bigfoot swung the tree over his head, making it whistle through the air.

"You should go inside," Blue told her. "It isn't safe for you out here."

"I will," said Cory, but she was so interested that she couldn't move. Then the Bigfoot let go of the tree and she found herself on the porch where Blue had set her.

Cory hurried to the railing to get a better view of the Bigfoot. The creature was only a little taller than the ogres and was covered with so much long, shaggy brown fur that it was hard to see his face. His movements were clumsy, and he shambled rather than ran.

Cory watched as he came at the ogres who were standing between him and the house. Swinging with his right arm, he punched Skweely with so much force that Cory heard the thud. Skweely took half a step backward but held his ground. The Bigfoot roared again, loud enough to make the windows rattle in their frames. Blue ducked when the Bigfoot tried to punch him in the jaw. When the creature's own momentum kept turning him, Blue grabbed his other arm and jerked it behind him, knocking him off balance. The Bigfoot fell to his knees and the ogres piled on top of him, smashing him to the ground.

"Are you ready to give up?" asked Blue.

The Bigfoot grunted and tried to get up, but was unable to move. He started to thrash then, flailing his one free arm and kicking his feet until the ogres pinned those down, too.

"You ready now?" Macks asked. The Bigfoot panted from his efforts. Gathering his strength, he tried to heave them off one last time. The pile of ogres rose about a foot, then collapsed back on him.

Cory was surprised when the Bigfoot began to laugh. "Well, ain't this something else! I never fought ogres before. You guys are strong! When I saw y'all standing there, I thought, *Melter, what have you gotten yourself into?* Do you mind gettin' up? I got a rock bigger 'n' my backside diggin' into me. Don't y'all worry none. I ain't gonna try to bother that little girl up on the porch anymore, you can take my word for it."

One by one the ogres stood up, leaving Melter lying on the ground. Then Blue offered him his hand and pulled him to his feet, and they all stood around, grinning like fools.

"I hate to say it, but that was fun! Ain't nobody give me a tussle like that before! Most often people see me and run away. What's the fun in that?"

"That happens to me all the time," said Twark. "Of course, they're usually screaming."

"That happened to me just the other day, didn't it, Cory?" said Macks.

"It did," Cory replied. "When we went to talk to Rina."

Melter dug a leaf out of his fur and looked at it. "Cory Feathering. Yep, that's the one I was supposed to scare. What did you do to get the guilds in such a tizzy?"

"I quit the Tooth Fairy Guild and they don't like it," Cory told him.

"Well, don't that beat all! They sent a Bigfoot after a tooth fairy! I can't wait to tell my buddies back home."

"Former tooth fairy," said Cory.

"Say, I'm hungry. Do y'all know of a good place to eat around here?" asked Melter.

"I think we're all hungry," Cory said, glancing at the ogres. "I was going to make sandwiches for lunch. Would you like to join us?"

"Sure! I'll eat just about anything, and hope that there's plenty of it. Thanks for the invitation!"

"It's our pleasure," Cory said as Blue took her hand. "It isn't every day that we get to entertain a Bigfoot."

CHAPTER
11

*I*tchy Butt's birthday party was being held on the shore of Turquoise Lake. Olot had told them to come early in case he needed help setting up, but by the time Cory's group arrived, Zephyr's new assistant had taken care of everything. Dillert had situated the stand close to the water's edge. Although he had done a good job, he had set it up in reverse, as if he had held a diagram backward. Cory's drums were usually set up on the left side of a stage. Today she would be playing on the right, closest to the water. No one else seemed to mind, so she didn't protest, either. It was Dillert's first day, after all.

A big tent had been set up farther down the lake, and caterers were putting out food when Cory, Blue, and the ogres went to investigate. "These are Itchy Butt's favorite foods," one of the caterers told them.

They saw pork rinds and frog rinds, pickled walrus flippers and pickled pigs' feet. Blue pointed out an elf chef standing at one end of the tent. "He's very well known," said Blue, "but I can't remember his name." When they walked over to see what he was doing, they found him basting squirrels on a rotisserie.

The sight and the smell combined were more than Cory could stand. Putting her hand over her mouth, she turned and hurried away. "I know ogres like meat, but I couldn't eat any of that," she told Blue when he caught up.

"I'm sure the caterers have something else," Blue told her. "I'll ask them."

"Not yet," Cory told him. "I think Olot wants me to come back now." She had caught a glimpse of Olot standing by the stage, waving them over. Another ogre was standing with him, and it was one she recognized. Cory had met Itchy Butt on a pedal-bus once. They hadn't talked much, but it had been enough to leave an impression.

The party guests had started to arrive, and they were already in a partying mood. It took Cory and Blue a few minutes to work their way through the crowd because so many people recognized them and wanted to say hello. When Cory and Blue finally made it to the stage, Olot started to introduce them.

"We've already met," Cory said, and smiled at Itchy Butt.

His wide mouth split into an enormous grin. "We sure did!" he said. "I wasn't sure a famous person like you would remember." Reaching out with one of his enormous hands, he slapped Cory on the back. What might have been considered a friendly tap to another ogre sent Cory flying. Blue caught her before she hit the ground, and he was frowning when he turned back to Itchy Butt.

"I'm so sorry!" the ogre declared, his face turning red. "I didn't mean to do that! Are you okay?"

The air had been knocked out of Cory, so it took a moment before she could speak. She nodded and squeezed Blue's arm, not wanting him to do something he'd later regret. "I'm fine," she finally gasped.

"Itchy Butt wants us to start playing as soon as we can," Olot hurried to say. "Are you ready, Cory?"

Cory knew he really meant, "Are you all right?" so she nodded and started toward her drums. Blue went with her; Macks, Skweely, and Twark were close behind.

"It looks like we might have to protect you from more than just the guilds," Blue said before Cory could climb onto the stage.

"It was an accident," she told him. "I'm sure Itchy Butt didn't mean it."

"Then we'll have to watch out for accidents, too," said Blue, and the three ogres nodded. "We'll stay right here, just in case."

While the other members of Zephyr started to warm up, Cory climbed onto the stage and picked up her drumsticks. Her back was sore where the ogre had slapped her, but that wouldn't stop her from playing.

When the band members had finished warming up, Olot started them with "Heat Lightning," which the ogres really enjoyed. They played "Shooting Stars" next, following it with "June Bug Jamboree." The song started out with an even tempo, but soon became as lively as if people really were swatting june bugs. Cory was whaling on her drums when an ogress started screaming. People often got so drawn into the music that they shouted and stomped their feet, so Cory didn't pay it much attention. She barely noticed as more party guests began to scream. Even when a shadow loomed over her, she kept playing. It wasn't until the other band members stopped playing and fled the stage that Cory noticed the water dripping on her drums. She faltered and looked up. Cold black eyes in a long narrow head looked down on her. The head itself was as big as she was tall, and she gasped when it started to draw nearer as the monster's long, sinuous neck rose farther from the water. Cory barely heard the shouts of Blue and his ogre friends as the monster's mouth opened so wide that she could see down its gullet. The odor of decaying fish was strong enough to make her gag. And then the mouth was almost on her and Blue was knocking her to the stage, covering her with his own body.

The creature was only feet away when it jerked and turned aside. Cory peered out from under Blue. Macks seemed to be fighting the band's new assistant, Dillert, while Skweely and Twark threw rocks at the monster. And then the other ogres at the party joined in, hurling rocks, sticks, empty bottles, and partly chewed cooked squirrel.

The monster roared a deep, throaty sound that reminded Cory of the water rushing over the cliff at Misty Falls. Blue was helping her up when the monster swung its head back toward them. "When I say 'go,' I want you to run as fast as you can away from the lake," said Blue.

"What about you?" asked Cory.

"Don't worry about me," said Blue. "I'll be fine as long as you're safe. Ready? Go!!"

Cory jumped from the stage and took off running, glancing over her shoulder every few yards. When the monster saw her, it roared again, its breath knocking over the drums that had remained upright on the stage. It was stretching its neck, trying to reach Cory, when

Blue and Macks jumped onto it. A moment later, Twark, Skweely, and some of the party guests joined them, clinging to the monster's neck like limpets as it tried to shake them off.

Cory had stopped halfway to the parking lot to see what was happening. When she saw the monster raise its head high, then turn and plunge into the water, she shouted, "Blue!" and ran back to the lake's edge.

Bubbles rose to the surface as the monster dove deep. Everyone gathered at the shore, watching the water and waiting for the monster to return. When nothing happened, Cory feared that Blue might have drowned. And then he erupted from the lake with the ogres close behind, cheering and slapping the water in sheer joy.

Cory waited while they began the swim to shore. "What happened?" she asked as they trudged out of the water.

"When the monster couldn't get rid of us, it gave up and went home," said Macks.

"Does it live on the bottom of the lake?" Cory asked Blue.

"I don't think so," said Blue, "but it definitely went somewhere. It was there one minute and gone the next. It disappeared right out from under us."

"What *was* that thing?" asked Cory.

"If it's what I think it is, it's got a lot of names. In the human world it's called Chessie or the Loch Ness Monster," Blue told her. "Here it's called Old Gnarly. My bet is it's one of the ITG's Big Baddies."

"Yeah," said Macks. "And so is that guy who works for Zephyr. A bad one, I mean, not a big one. He tried to stop us from helping you."

"I saw him throw something in the water right before the monster showed up," Twark said.

Blue frowned. "It was probably a signal for Old Gnarly to attack you. We need to tell Olot."

"You can tell him, but I wouldn't bother looking for that guy around here," said Skweely. "The last I saw of him, he was running for the parking lot."

"That was great!" Itchy Butt said as he joined them. "How did you arrange that monster thing?"

"We didn't arrange that," said Blue. "The attack was real."

"That's even better!" Itchy Butt exclaimed. "I can't wait to tell my friends. This is the best party ever! Say, are you going to finish your concert? You didn't even play the whole third song, and we're paying you for at least eight."

Cory glanced at Blue, then at her friends who were on the stage, inspecting their instruments. "We'll let you know," she said, and left Blue with his friends.

After checking her drums, and finding that they were only a little damp, Cory agreed with the other members of Zephyr that they could keep playing. This time they skipped "June Bug Jamboree" and went straight to their new song, "Summer Heat." Cory noticed that Blue and his ogre friends stayed even closer than before.

When they had played more than eight songs and responded to three standing ovations, Zephyr finally finished playing. Cory and her friends packed up their instruments while Blue told Olot about Dillert and the monster. By the time Cory finished getting her drums ready for Olot to move, the ogres had set up the games. She joined Blue at the sidelines to watch as Itchy Butt and his guests played a wild game of pin-the-tail-on-the-ogre tag. It was getting dark when the ogres brought out a big tub and filled it with water. When they started taking turns bobbing for rats' heads, Cory turned to Blue. "Do you mind if we leave now?" she asked.

"I thought you'd never ask," he replied.

The three ogres who had come with them wanted to stay at the party, so Cory and Blue said good-bye to Chancy, Olot, and the other members of Zephyr. They were heading to the parking lot when a firefly works display began at the other end of the lake.

"How beautiful!" Cory said, watching the night sky where thousands of fireflies were synchronizing their flashes, creating pictures and designs in light. "Would you mind if we go watch it? I'd love to see the show."

"Sure," said Blue. "I've always liked firefly works."

They rode the solar cycle around the lake, parking at the end of a long row of cycles. The ground by the lake was covered with people reclining on blankets, staring up at the sky. They were so caught up in the show that Cory wasn't worried someone might recognize her.

Cory had no idea how the fireflies did it, but they were able to change their color as well as the duration of their flashes. When they created pictures of flowers, the flower fairies cried out in admiration. Frost fairies applauded when giant snowflakes appeared in the night sky. There were images of unicorns and dragons, butterflies and songbirds. Each one seemed better than the last.

The show was approaching its grand finale when Blue said, "We should leave now or we'll get stuck in traffic."

Smiling, Cory nodded and took his hand, her eyes shining with all the wonderful things she'd seen. Her smile faded when she heard a woman's voice call out, "Look who's here! If it isn't my wayward daughter! Out for a wild night on the town, Cory?"

Blue's grip tightened on Cory's hand as she turned around. "Hello, Mother," she said.

Delphinium was there with three other women who were all looking at Cory with open curiosity. "I didn't expect to see you here," said Cory's mother. "I would have thought you'd be hiding in your uncle's house."

"I would have thought you'd be at work, collecting children's teeth," Cory replied.

"I'm no longer working in the field," said Delphinium. "Mary Mary appointed me to the Tooth Fairy Guild Advisory Board."

"It sounds as if things are going well for you," Cory said.

"They are. You would know all about it if you ever stopped by."

Cory thought her mother looked wistful for a moment, but the moment passed and Delphinium's expression turned bitter. "You might have been able to hold a position of authority someday, too, if you hadn't squandered your valuable training."

The grand finale started, lighting the sky with a gorgeous bouquet of firefly flowers. Blue squeezed Cory's hand. "Excuse us, but we should be going," he told Delphinium.

"Good night, Mother," Cory told her before walking away.

"That wasn't too terrible," Blue told Cory as they hurried to the cycle. "I got the impression that she really does miss you. I bet she's been dying to tell you about her appointment to the board."

Cory shrugged. "Maybe." *And maybe someday, when this mess with the guilds is over, I might actually go see her,* Cory thought.

They had almost reached the cycle when Cory spotted Mary Lambkin and Jasper Wilkins, who were also leaving the park.

"Cory!" Mary called. "You're just the person I wanted to see. You were right! Jasper and I are perfect for each other. We're going to my parents' house in New Town in a few days to get married, then on to the shore for our honeymoon. Thank you so much for bringing us together. We never would have met if it weren't for you. Please feel free to use my name if you ever need a matchmaking reference."

"You're welcome!" said Cory. "I'm glad it all worked out."

Cory was thrilled that Mary and Jasper were so happy together. She thought about them as she put on her helmet and climbed onto the cycle behind Blue. She was still thinking about them as she and Blue rode down the street. If only she could make more couples just as happy. No one had contacted her about matchmaking after the guilds got truly nasty, and she found that she missed making matches. Wondering who else she could match, she thought about the one couple whose images kept appearing in her mind. Because she had no intention of matching her mother and Officer Deeds, she decided that they didn't count. But there was one other couple she could match. It wasn't that long ago that she had seen Micah's true love.

Closing her eyes, Cory thought about her uncle. His match popped into her head right away. It was a fairy woman with curly pink hair, vivid green eyes, and a quirky smile that made her seem friendly. *I should find her*, Cory thought. *Micah has been so good to me. He deserves true love if anyone does.*

It was late when they finally walked in the door, so Cory was surprised to find her uncle sitting in the main room, reading a book. "I couldn't sleep," he said when she asked. "I tried, but I lay awake worrying about all sorts of things, so I got up and found a good book."

Cory remembered what her grandfather had said that very morning. "I have an idea that might help you," she told Micah. "According to my grandfather, the monster who came here last night can make everyone in a household worry. He told me what to do about it. Stay where you are, Micah, and Blue, you sit over there."

While Blue took a seat, Cory walked around the room, turning out the fairy lights. When it was dark, she thought, *Wings!* and they sprouted from between her shoulder blades as if they'd always been there. "He told me to think about love," she said to herself. Closing her eyes, she thought about how much she loved Blue, how happy she was when he was around, and how she wanted to spend the rest of her life with him. She thought about her uncle and how kind he had been to her, how she had always loved him, and how much she wanted him to be happy. She thought about her friends and how she loved them, too, even when they drove her a little crazy. Each time she thought about a different kind of love, she felt warmer inside.

"Wow!" Blue murmured. "Would you look at that!"

Cory opened her eyes, wondering if he was teasing her. She was standing with her wings spread wide like her grandfather had suggested. Without thinking about it, she had spread her arms, too, as if she was offering someone a hug. Her head was tilted back, so that she was looking at the ceiling. However, the strangest and most unexpected thing was that she was glowing. A soft, rosy light was coming from her body, her face, and even her hair. When she glanced at her arms, she thought they didn't look real.

"That's incredible!" said Blue. "I know I feel better."

"I don't know about you, but I'm not worried at all now," her uncle said with a laugh. "With that kind of ability on our side, I don't think any of us have a thing to worry about!"

CHAPTER
12

The next day, Cory received a message from Jonas McDonald.

Cory,
    I really like your baby dragon, but she can no longer live here with me. Please come get her.
                         Jonas McDonald

Cory's heart sank. After Princess Lillian gave her the baby dragon, Cory had hoped to keep it with her at Micah's. When that didn't work out, she had given Shimmer to Jonas McDonald to help with his fairy problem. Cory had thought she'd found a good permanent home for the dragon at McDonald's farm, so she was surprised to get his message. Now she didn't know what to do.

Thinking about each of her friends, she tried to come up with someone who would be glad to give a home to a dragon. It would have to be someone who liked animals and had a fireproof house. There was only one person she thought she could ask.

Olot,
      Would you and Chancy be able to give a home to a baby dragon? She is very cute and her name is Shimmer.
                                   Cory

Olot's reply came just a few minutes later.

Cory,
      I've never had a pet dragon! Sure! Bring her with you when you come to tonight's rehearsal.
                                   Olot

Pleased that it was settled, Cory told Macks that they were going to the Dell, the farm that had belonged to the McDonald family for years.

"It's been a long time since I went for a ride in the

country," said Macks. "A little peace and quiet will be restful after all that excitement yesterday."

"Did you have fun at the party after Blue and I left?" Cory asked him as they stepped onto the porch.

"I sure did," said Macks. "But wrestling with a Bigfoot and Old Gnarly on the same day made it the best day ever!"

They both enjoyed the ride through the open countryside. Cory was surprised that Macks could identify all the crops and animal breeds. "My parents lived in town, but I spent most of my summers at Blue's house," Macks told her. "We were always getting into trouble. Boy, did we have fun!"

When they arrived at the Dell, Jonas McDonald was picking grapes to take to the market. Cory saw him from up by the house, but he didn't seem to hear her when she called to him. Glad that she'd worn sensible shoes, Cory and Macks hiked back to where Jonas was working. When they got closer, Cory tried again. When Jonas didn't respond, she kept walking toward him, waving her arms while shouting, "Jonas! Hey, Jonas, we're here!"

She must have caught his eye, because he turned their way and was startled when he saw them. "Sorry!" he said as he pulled earplugs out of his ears. "I wear these so I don't hear the screaming."

Cory was close enough now that she could hear the gossiping grapes shouting and talking in their tiny, high-pitched voices. The grapes were the result of repeated accidental sprinklings of fairy dust by passing flower fairies. Although the dust had altered most of the produce on the farm, the grapes were the most obnoxious. Jonas had contacted Cory to help with the problem. Shimmer had been her answer.

"The grapes scream when I pick them," Jonas said, plucking one from the vine as he said it. When the grape screamed like a frightened baby, Cory could understand the earplugs.

"It really gets on my nerves after a couple of minutes," said Jonas. "I took your suggestion and sold them as a novelty at the market, but you can only sell so many of these before people aren't interested anymore. I want my old kind of grapes back. I'm hoping that next season the vines will produce normal grapes again."

"Did Shimmer help at all?" asked Cory.

"She sure did! The fairies changed their flight pattern after Shimmer chased them off. They don't fly over my farm at all anymore," said Jonas. "But, well, come here and I'll show you."

He led them down the path to another part of the farm where cornstalks grew chest high. Most of them looked strong and healthy, but a large section had been burned to the ground.

"Shimmer gets a little excited sometimes and isn't very good at controlling her flame," Jonas explained. "I'm sure she'll get better at it as she gets older, but I can't wait that long. This isn't the only burned patch around the farm. There are others even bigger than this. I need you to take her home today while I still have some produce to sell."

"I already have a new home for her," said Cory. "I'm sorry it ended this way."

"So am I. That little dragon is really friendly and nice to have around. I'm sorry I can't keep her. By the way, you set me up on a date with that girl, Goldilocks. I saw in the paper where she married Prince Rupert. She was nice, but not right for me. Any chance you know any other girls who might want to go out?"

Cory closed her eyes and *saw* Jonas in her mind, but no one else appeared beside him. That didn't mean she couldn't set him up on a date, however. Daisy was between boyfriends, and it was about time she went out with a good person.

"Actually, I think I do," Cory told him. "I'll see what I can arrange."

"Great!" Jonas said, his eyes lighting up. "I'll get Shimmer. She's taking a nap in the shed behind the house. I tried keeping her inside the house, but my dogs are terrified of her."

Cory understood why Jonas had put Shimmer in a shed when she saw that it was made of cement blocks. What was left of the burned door was standing open so that sunlight fell on the baby dragon sleeping in a pile of hay.

"Shimmer!" Cory said, kneeling just outside the door. "I'm taking you with me."

The little dragon opened sleepy eyes and blinked. When she launched herself at Cory, Macks shouted and tried to grab Shimmer, but Cory hugged her, delighted that the dragon seemed so happy to see her.

"She really belongs to you," said Jonas. "She's never been that happy to see me. Are you sure you can't keep her yourself?"

"I wish I could," Cory said, and hugged the dragon a little harder.

"You didn't tell me that we were picking up a dragon," Macks said as they walked to his solar cycle. "Where are we going to put her to get her home? You can't put her in the compartment. There wouldn't be enough air."

Cory was carrying the little dragon in her arms. "I hadn't thought of that," she said, scratching Shimmer's head. "I rode the pedal-bus here and carried her in the basket, but she's grown since then. She's really smart, though. I wonder . . . Macks, go ahead and get on the cycle. I'll be right there."

Setting Shimmer on the ground, Cory knelt beside her and said, "We're going to my uncle's house now. We want you to go with us, too. It's a long way to fly, but I think you could make it. We'll stop now and then so you can rest. Will you fly above the cycle and stay with us?"

The little dragon didn't say anything, but then Cory didn't expect her to. She wasn't a talking animal like Weegie, after all. However, Cory knew Shimmer was smarter than Noodles and maybe smarter than Weegie. If the two woodchucks could do all the things they did, surely the little dragon could follow her home.

When Cory walked to the cycle, Shimmer ran along after her. She continued to run, crying, even after they started down the road.

"Fly, Shimmer!" cried Cory. "I know you can do it!"

Shimmer ran a few steps farther and stopped. She looked so pitiful that Cory was thinking about having Macks turn around when suddenly the little dragon launched herself into the air.

"Come on, Shimmer!" Cory cried, and was delighted when the dragon began to follow them. Seeing a flying dragon was always a thrilling sight, but especially when it was exactly where you wanted it to be.

It was midafternoon when they finally returned home. Cory called to Shimmer and the baby dragon flew straight to her, making happy little chirruping sounds. Wanita was struggling to drag a reluctant Boris home from the park when Cory started up the walk, carrying Shimmer. The little dragon puffed hot air at the boar, who sniffed and bolted for home, dragging Wanita behind him.

"Showing the neighbors who's boss, huh?" Cory said as she petted Shimmer.

As soon as they were inside, Shimmer settled back in as if she'd never left. Cory gave her the dishes she'd used before and put her bed back in the kitchen, where it had gone when she first brought Shimmer home from Misty Falls. Tired from flying, the little dragon curled up on the bed while Cory fetched some books from the main room. It was time to make another match.

Cory had *seen* her uncle's match, but had no idea who the fairy was or where to find her. Like she often did when trying to find a fairy whose face she had *seen*, Cory started her search by going through her uncle's collection of old yearbooks. If the fairy had gone to Junior Fey School, her picture should be there.

Cory looked through the books page by page while Macks came in for a drink and left; Shimmer woke up, turned over, and went back to sleep; and Noodles scratched at the door to go out. She finally found the picture in a yearbook that was ten years older than her own. Quince Brookfield was eleven years younger than Micah.

It helped to have a name to match the face, but Cory still had a lot to learn about the fairy. Quince had been a general education major, which meant that she hadn't trained in any specific field. This made finding her a lot harder. Hoping to learn where Quince worked, Cory began going through the few lists that she had. One list included all the people who worked in the town government. Quince was not on the list. Some of the guilds had recently made public partial lists of guild members. Quince didn't seem to be on any of those lists, either.

Cory had just finished going through yet another list when Macks walked into the kitchen. "What are you doing?" he asked, peeking over her shoulder.

"I'm looking for someone named Quince Brookfield," said Cory. "But I haven't had any luck so far. Have you ever heard of her?"

Macks shook his head. "If you can't find her in the usual places, she might have a nontraditional kind of job."

"I thought of that," Cory said. "So how do I find her?"

"I have no idea," said Macks. "People in those kinds of jobs don't usually have their names on lists."

Cory was still looking for Quince's name when she realized that it was almost time to leave for rehearsal. After putting the papers away, she made a quick salad and was just getting out the dishes when Blue arrived. They ate after Macks left, and were soon on the road themselves. This time Cory wore a pack on her back that could hold the little dragon, which Shimmer really seemed to like.

When they reached Olot's cave, the ogre and his wife took to Shimmer right away. Olot declared that she could have the run of the cave, as long as she was a good girl, and Chancy showed her the bed she'd already made up. Shimmer was a big hit with all the band members, too, and Skippy's girlfriends spent the entire rehearsal cooing over her and admiring her scales.

When the band had finished practicing for the night, Olot said that he had an announcement. "As I'm sure you all know by now, our assistant, Dillert, was working against us at the last performance. Since then, I have looked into him more thoroughly, which I admit I should have done before hiring him. I learned that Dillert is an enforcer for the Flower Fairy Guild and not unaffiliated as he claimed when I met him."

"What does an enforcer do?" one of Skippy's girl-friends called out.

"He's one of the people who do the guild's secret dirty work," said Olot. "That means he was exactly the kind of person that we didn't want. Zephyr is once again looking for someone to fill Goldilocks's position. This time we will look into the applicant thoroughly. If you know of anyone who might be suitable, please have him contact me."

"May I suggest that you consider hiring an ogre?" Blue said. "They have no guild affiliations; they are strong, hard workers; and you and I both know a number of good ogres who would do an excellent job."

"That's true!" said Olot. "I should have thought of that myself. I'll look into it right away. And that reminds me; I have one more announcement tonight. Although our regular venues aren't hiring us now, we are getting a lot of requests from the ogre community. We were a big hit at Itchy Butt's party and word has spread. Ogres aren't afraid of the guilds, and are eager to have us perform at their events. I'm in negotiations with a number of ogres now, and will let you know more at our next rehearsal. If you have any questions or comments, come see me."

While Cheeble, Skippy, and Perky crowded around Olot, vying to talk to him first, Daisy headed for the door. Cory hurried to stop her. "Before you go, I need to talk to you for just a minute. You don't have a new boyfriend yet, do you?"

"No, I don't," said Daisy. "And I don't know if I ever will. My heart has been broken too many times. It may never heal."

"That's too bad," said Cory. "Because I know a very nice young man who I think you'd really like. He's not a member of any guild so he wouldn't have any ulterior motives, but if you aren't interested . . ."

"What's his name?" Daisy asked, her pointed ears perking up.

"Jonas McDonald. He owns his own farm and has his own house and—"

"Is he a fairy?"

"He's a human, actually. You said you'd dated a human before," said Cory.

"I did, years ago. Some humans are very nice. What does he look like?"

"Tall and handsome," Cory told her.

"All right then," said Daisy. "I might as well jump back into the dating pond. When can you set it up?"

"Would tomorrow be too soon?" asked Cory. "Your poor heart—"

"Can handle it just fine," said Daisy. "Send me a message as soon as you know where and when. I'll be ready!"

"That was easy," Cory told Blue as Daisy started down the hall. "But then Daisy never has been happy unless she has a boyfriend."

"Uh-huh," Blue said, looking distracted. "Listen, when we go outside, you stay in the doorway while I get the cycle and come back to pick you up. I don't want to give the guilds a chance to get to you."

"Just be careful," Cory said, seeing the concern in Blue's eyes.

"I will," said Blue. "And you be ready to get on the cycle as fast as you can. There's no telling what might be on this mountainside at night."

While Blue hurried to get the cycle, Cory stood in the doorway, peering out into the dark. The light from the hallway did little to illuminate the trees and under-brush just yards away. She jumped when she heard something in the branches overhead. Although she started to back into the cave, she wasn't fast enough. A dark shape plunged from a branch and swooped down to grab Cory, sinking talons into her shoulders as it plucked her from the doorway and hauled her into the air. Pain shot through Cory as the creature tightened its grip.

Cory screamed as she struggled. Looking up, she couldn't see what was holding her until they were higher than the trees and the stars were twinkling above them.

Even then the figure was indistinct, although Cory could just make out tattered wings and a woman's face looking down at her. She could smell it now; the stench of harpy was enough to make her gag.

She heard shouting below her, but she doubted her friends could help. The harpy started to fly over the mountainside, taking Cory farther from Blue and her bandmates. Suddenly, a rock whistled past her, hitting the harpy's wing and making the creature miss a beat. The harpy flew higher, but she hadn't gone far when another rock hit her in the jaw. Startled, the harpy shrieked and let go of Cory. Cory was too dazed to react as she began to tumble from the sky. It had just occurred to her that she could use her wings when she slammed into something that dipped, then lifted her up again. Breathless, Cory turned her head to see Blue's worried face peering down at her.

"You caught me!" she cried, throwing her arms around him.

Blue nodded. "When I saw the harpy take you, I followed on my cycle. I've never pedaled so hard in my life! It's a good thing harpies can't fly very fast. Are you all right? Your shirt is wet and . . . Cory, you're bleeding!"

"I'll be fine," Cory assured him. "The harpy dug her talons into my shoulders."

"Is Cory all right?" Olot called, puffing as he ran up with Skippy close behind. "When I threw that rock, I didn't think the harpy would drop her like that."

"She's bleeding from the harpy's talons. I've heard those things are filthy," Blue told him.

"Bring her back to the cave," said Olot. "Chancy can take a look. She knows all about herbal medicine from her days in the wicked queen's castle."

"Are you able to sit on the cycle?" Blue asked Cory. "I can get you there faster that way."

"I think so," Cory said, although the pain was nearly as strong as when the harpy had been carrying her.

Blue carried her to the cycle and set her down as if she were made of glass. She wrapped her arms around him and held on as best she could, but her arms were shaking and didn't have much strength. When they reached the cave, Blue carried her inside and set her on the sofa.

"What happened?" Chancy cried.

Cory closed her eyes while Blue explained, and didn't open them again until she felt Chancy peel back her shirt and start washing the wounds in her shoulders with warm water. "Here, drink this," Blue told her, holding a cup to her lips.

Cory did, although it tasted nasty.

"I learned a lot about harpies when I worked in the wicked queen's castle," said Chancy as she dabbed at the wounds. "She had three in her palace guard. Nasty creatures, and very self-centered. They didn't care that maids had to follow them around, cleaning up after them every minute of the day just so the castle wouldn't reek. One of them scratched my friend Gloria by accident. I was the one to nurse Gloria back to health, so I know what I'm doing. I'm going to put some salve on these. It will sting at first, but then it should feel a whole lot better. The tonic you just drank will help keep you from getting an infection."

Cory nodded and closed her eyes again. She clenched her teeth as Chancy spread the salve. At first the salve just made the pain worse, but within seconds the pain faded to a dull ache.

"Thank you," she said as Chancy covered the wounds with salve-coated leaves.

"You're welcome," Chancy told her. "You should be completely healed in a few days."

"Is she able to go home now, or should she stay here awhile?" Blue asked Chancy.

"I want to go home," Cory declared.

When Chancy nodded, Blue slid his hands under Cory and picked her up. "I can walk, you know," she told him.

"Not until I get you home," he said as he started toward the door.

After carrying her to the cycle, he set her on the seat and put her helmet on for her. Moments later they were on their way down the path to the road that led around the mountainside.

"So far, so good," said Blue. "I know you're hurting, but can you keep an eye on the trees? I have to look for holes in the road."

"At least the stars are out," said Cory. "That should help a little bit and I—Watch out! There's something coming toward the road from the right!"

Blue pedaled faster, swerving to the left. Cory watched wide-eyed as a big creature covered with long, white fur thundered toward the road, no longer trying to be quiet. She could see its red eyes only yards away as it tore down the mountainside, reaching the road only moments after they'd passed by. It roared in frustration, and Cory could feel the road shake as it kept coming.

Blue pedaled as fast as he could up and over a rise in the road. And then they were on the downhill slope and it felt as if they were flying. With Blue's feet off the pedals, they glided down the mountainside, racing faster than the creature following them could run. When the road finally leveled off, they had left the creature far behind.

"That was another Big Baddie, I suppose," Cory said once they felt safe enough to slow down.

"I caught just a glimpse, but I think that was a yeti," Blue told her. "They live high in the snowy mountains to the north. I'll send messages to Olot and the pigs when we get back to Micah's. They should know what's lurking around their caves. And you need to go straight to bed. You must be exhausted."

"I will," Cory said, although she doubted the ache in her shoulders was going to make sleeping easy.

CHAPTER
13

Cory slept better than she thought she would, and woke feeling nearly normal the next day. When she checked her wounds in the mirror, they looked as if they had almost healed. "How are you feeling?" Blue asked when she walked into the kitchen.

"Great!" Cory said.

"You should still take it easy today," Blue told her.

"I really don't think I need to," said Cory. "Look!"

When she showed him one of her shoulders, even Blue had to admit that the salve had done its job.

After a breakfast of toast and fruit juice, Cory arranged for Daisy and Jonas to have supper at Everything Leeks. She had just stepped outside when Weegie staggered up, saying, "My back is killing me! I think it might be broken. Did you see the size of the monster that stepped on me?"

"I did," Cory told her. "He was smaller than I am. And if your back was broken, you probably wouldn't be able to move."

"All I want is a little sympathy," grumbled Weegie. "Is that too much to ask? And that monster was bigger than you when he stepped on me! He shrank after your uncle turned all the lights on. Ooh! It hurts! I'm dying!"

"Do you want to go to the doctor?" Cory asked. "I can send a message to get an appointment."

"If you think that would help," Weegie said, sounding pitiful.

Cory sighed. Having two woodchucks in the house wasn't easy. It was even harder when one of them was so dramatic.

Cory was able to get an appointment for Weegie, but they could take her only if she came right away. Although Blue offered to give her a ride on his way to work, Macks showed up before they stepped out the door.

Cory had taken Noodles to see Dr. Dickory once before when the woodchuck had swallowed twine from Micah's garden shed. She had taken the pedal-bus then and carried Noodles in the basket. This time she rode with Macks and had the woodchuck ride in a basket that the ogre strapped to the back of his cycle. The woodchuck wasn't comfortable, but it was the best Cory could do.

There were four animals ahead of them in the waiting room when they arrived. A flower fairy was cradling a frightened chipmunk in her arms, glaring at the black leopard that Cory recognized right away.

"Hi, Selene! Felice, what's wrong with your sister?" Cory asked the brown-haired girl sitting on the bench behind the leopard.

"Nothing," said Felice as Selene began to purr. "We're here for our checkups."

The big cat's loud rumble seemed to frighten the chipmunk even more. Squeaking, it ran up its owner's sleeve.

A little girl with long, blond pigtails was sitting in the corner with her mother. When a bright red snake poked its head out of the basket she was holding, the girl said, "Not now, Ruby," and poked it back in.

While Cory signed in at the front counter, Macks took a seat beside a tall, thin man with a nervous white rabbit on a leash. "It's okay, buddy," the man kept assuring the rabbit. "Our turn is next."

"Mr. Carroll!" called the elf maiden behind the counter. "The doctor will see Mr. Rabbit now."

When the man took his rabbit into the examining room, Cory sat in the seat beside Macks. Taking off the knapsack, she found Weegie curled up in a ball, asleep. Cory didn't want to disturb her, so she left her there and held the knapsack on her lap.

Mr. Carroll and his rabbit weren't in the examining room long before he came out looking worried. Selene and Felice were called in next. Macks fell asleep soon after that, so Cory started reading old issues of *The Fey Express*. Other than Selene and Felice, she barely noticed who came and went. She was about to fall asleep herself when the elf maiden finally called her name.

Weegie woke with a start when Cory stood up, and was moaning about her back again when Cory and Macks walked into the examining room. The woodchuck started telling Dr. Dickory all about it as soon as she saw him. Cory held the woodchuck's paw while the doctor examined her. When he was done, Dr. Dickory shook his head and said, "I'm afraid there isn't a thing I can do."

"You mean I'm going to die?" Weegie squealed.

"No, of course not!" said the doctor. "I mean you shouldn't be here. What you need is an animal chiropractor. Your back is out of alignment and a chiropractor can fix it. I believe there's one around the corner. Fur and Feathers Chiropractic, or something like that."

"Do you mean to say that we waited in your waiting room all that time just so we can go wait in another waiting room?" grumbled Macks.

The doctor shrugged. "Looks that way."

"This isn't right," Macks announced as Cory urged him out the door.

"It is what it is," Cory said, ignoring all the curious faces in the waiting room.

They found Fur and Feathers easily enough because it really was right around the corner. This time there were only two people in the waiting room. Two gnomes, one male and one female, had brought in a pure white deer with silver antlers. He was a beautiful animal with a regal quality that even Weegie seemed to notice. She kept quiet as long as the deer was there, but the moment he went to another room, the woodchuck began to complain about her back again.

Cory and Macks didn't have long to wait before they were called as well. A middle-aged human woman showed them to the next room, which was empty when they arrived. Only a few minutes passed before the door opened and the chiropractor walked in. "I'm Quince Brookfield," she said. "What seems to be the problem?"

Cory's mouth opened, but no words came out. "Hey!" said Macks. "Isn't that the name of—Oof!" Cory elbowed him hard in the stomach before he could say any more.

Fortunately, Weegie was already taking charge of the conversation, giving Cory time to study her uncle's match. Quince had curly pink hair and vivid green eyes just like in her picture, but where she had looked young and cheerful, she now looked older and a little tired. Cory watched as Quince examined Weegie, noting her long, elegant fingers and how gentle she was with the woodchuck.

At first Cory was delighted to have found her uncle's match, but she soon started to worry. Unlike all the other matches Cory had made, this one would affect her directly. If Micah married Quince, she would move into his house. Cory had no intention of staying there if that happened. She had no choice; she would have to move out, but the question was, where should she go? Her grandfather had made a very kind offer, but should she really take him up on it? Knowing how awful the guilds could be, did she really want to bring it all down on Lionel? Micah had handled it very well, but then he wasn't as old as Lionel, nor did he have such a big secret to hide. If the guilds were snooping around Lionel's house, how long would it be before they discovered that he was a Cupid?

The important thing is Micah's happiness, she reminded herself. *I'll have to figure something out.*

Cory was still turning this over in her mind when she realized that Quince was talking to her. ". . . back tomorrow. I think she'll be fine with one more treatment. If that works for you, you can schedule tomorrow's appointment on your way out."

Cory thought that was perfect. Micah could come with her and she could shoot them both.

"Thank you," she said out loud as Macks picked up Weegie. "She looks better already."

Cory didn't feel like talking on the drive home. Instead, she mulled over her options. She could find a place of her own, although she really didn't like the thought of living by herself, or she could accept her grandfather's offer. She was still thinking about what she should do when Macks pulled up in front of Micah's house.

"You seem upset," he said as he took Weegie out of the basket. "Is something wrong?"

Cory shook her head. "No, everything is fine. I just need to make a few decisions."

She spent most of the day thinking while she cleaned. She started a load of laundry first, then scrubbed the bathing room. When it was spotless, she made a vegetable and cheese casserole before she began to clean the kitchen. If she was moving out, she wanted to leave it cleaner than when she'd moved in.

By the time Blue arrived, Cory knew what she had to do. She was hoping to talk to him before supper, but he was so preoccupied that she couldn't bring it up. Micah was home earlier than usual, which meant that there were three of them for supper. When Cory set the casserole on the table, Micah served himself, but Blue still seemed distracted. Even after he had food on his plate, he didn't seem interested in it. When he took a few bites and set down his fork, Cory finally asked, "What's wrong? Did something happen?"

"What? Oh, no," said Blue. "It's just the trial."

"Is it going against us?" Cory asked, setting down the pitcher she had just picked up.

"It's hard to say," said Blue. "And I'm not really supposed to talk about it."

"Surely you can tell us something!" Micah said.

Blue sighed and nodded. "I can't tell you anything specific, but I suppose I can tell you this much. Today they questioned the people who had harassed you, Cory. Tom Tom and Lewis the wolf were there. So were some flower fairies, a couple of frost fairies, and two members of the Housecleaning Guild. They couldn't deny what they had done, and everyone I talked to told me that it sounded awful in court. Normally I'd think that the trial was going our way. But the guilds have been spreading lies about you and a lot of people believe them. They're saying that you deserved to be treated the way you were. I just hope the jury doesn't agree with them."

"That doesn't sound good," said Micah.

"No, it doesn't," said Blue. "And the trial should be over soon."

Cory wasn't happy about his news, but she had something else to worry about now. "I took Weegie to the vet this morning. He sent us to the animal chiropractor for help with her back. We have another appointment tomorrow morning. I'd like it if you could both go with me. That way the chiropractor can show us all what we need to do for Weegie."

"Do I really need to go?" asked her uncle. "I didn't tell anyone that I needed to take off tomorrow."

"Couldn't you learn whatever it is and tell us about it tomorrow night?" Blue said.

Cory shook her head. "I really think it's important that you're both there. I got the first appointment of the day, so it shouldn't take too long."

Neither Blue nor her uncle looked happy about it, but Cory didn't care. They were going, and that's all she needed. Micah had to be there so she could make his match. She needed Blue because Macks couldn't take two passengers on his solar cycle. Although she hated lying for any reason, she couldn't tell them the truth, at least not now.

After supper, Cory and Blue had to hurry to leave for her rehearsal. They were on their way up the mountainside when Cory brought up the chiropractor again. "I couldn't tell you everything at supper because I didn't want Micah to know, but I found his true love and I'm going to make the match tomorrow. Her name is Quince Brookfield and she's Weegie's chiropractor."

Blue turned his head enough to ask, "Are you sure?"

"I *saw* her, so yes, I'm sure. I need you to go tomorrow so you can drive Micah there."

"This should be interesting," Blue said with a laugh. "Now that I know what it's about, I wouldn't miss this for anything!"

CHAPTER
14

Cory was dressed and ready to go before she went into the kitchen for breakfast the next morning. When she walked into the room, her uncle had propped a message against her plate.

Cory,
    Chancy and I really like Shimmer, but we are unable to keep her. Please be prepared to take her with you when you come to rehearsal tonight.
                                    Olot

"Oh, no," said Cory. "Not again!"

"What's wrong?" Blue asked as he set a platter of pancakes on the table.

"Olot can't keep Shimmer. Now I have to find another home for her! Do either of you know anyone who would be good to her and give her a good home?"

"I can put up a note in the teachers' lounge," said Micah.

"And I can ask around at the station," Blue told her.

"That's nice of you both. I hate the thought of giving her to a stranger," said Cory. "I hope it doesn't come to that."

Macks showed up just as they were finishing breakfast. Micah looked irritated when Cory reminded him of the chiropractor. "I already sent a message to the school office," he told her. "They expect me in as soon as I can make it."

"That's not a problem," Cory told him. When she saw that Blue was grinning like crazy, she almost wished she hadn't told him about what was really going to happen. Hoping that Micah wouldn't see his smile and get curious, she hurried them out the door and onto the solar cycles.

Cory rode to the chiropractor's office behind Blue while Micah rode behind Macks. Once again Weegie was curled up inside the knapsack, but this time she didn't fall asleep. Instead, she grumbled to herself, shifting around now and then as she tried to get comfortable.

They were parking their cycles when Micah glanced up at the chiropractor's sign. "Huh! The last time I was in this part of town, this was a cobbler's shop. A couple of nice brownies ran it; brothers, I think."

"The sign does look fairly new," Cory said as she led them to the door.

There was no one in the waiting room when they arrived, so they sat together where they could see the door into the inner rooms. Cory was just beginning to wonder if she should have brought a book to read when the door opened and a young woman gestured them in.

"I don't think you need me in there," said Macks. "I'll wait out here, if that's okay with you."

Cory nodded and the others filed in behind her. While Blue shut the door, Cory set Weegie on the examining table. Micah was studying the diplomas on the walls when Quince walked in. She was looking at Weegie as she approached the table and didn't notice Micah or Blue. Although Blue seemed mesmerized when she started to manipulate the woodchuck's muscles, Micah's eyes never left Quince's face. She didn't look up until she was finished.

Quince looked surprised when she saw Micah standing there. "Hello!" she said, her voice sounding odd.

"Hi!" Micah said in a softer voice than usual.

They paused then, neither saying anything as they gazed into each other's eyes. Cory could have sworn she felt an electric tingle for a moment and knew beyond a doubt that she was doing the right thing.

Bow! Cory thought as she reached out her hands. Time stood still for everyone else as a bow appeared in one hand, a quiver in the other. Taking one of the two arrows from the quiver, Cory read the name "Quince Blossom Brookfield" printed on the shaft. After nocking the arrow on the bowstring, she pulled the string back and let the arrow fly. It hit Quince's chest, releasing a shower of sparkles.

The next arrow read "Micah Oakwood Fleuren." When she let the arrow loose, it hit Micah so hard that he swayed on his feet. Sparks shot between Micah and Quince, obscuring them for a few seconds. Cory held out the bow and quiver, which disappeared just before Micah blinked.

"You're . . . ," Micah began.

"So are you," whispered Quince.

Cory grabbed Weegie off the table and got out of the way as Quince and Micah began to walk toward each other. They met by the end of the table where they fell into each other's arms as if magnets were pulling them.

"Thank you, Quince. We'll be going now if you're finished with Weegie," said Cory. "Uncle Micah, we have to go. Are you coming with us?"

Neither of them answered her, but then they were so busy gazing into each other's eyes that she didn't think they would. Blue was grinning like crazy again when they left the office.

"Isn't Micah coming?" Macks asked as they walked outside.

"He'll come home when he's ready," said Cory. "He has something else to take care of first."

"That was incredible!" Blue said as he got on his cycle. "Is it always like that?"

"Pretty much," Cory told him.

"So are you going to shoot me someday?" he whispered into her ear.

"Do I need to?" she whispered back.

Blue gazed into her eyes. "No, you don't. Our first kiss was enough to tie us together for life."

Leaning down from his seat on his cycle, he pulled Cory close and kissed her until she was breathless. When he let her go, she staggered back and bumped into Macks. "See that she gets home safe and sound, buddy," Blue told his friend. "She means everything to me."

Cory watched Blue ride off before getting on Macks's cycle. "What happened in that office?" Macks asked her. "Everyone was fine when you went in, then Micah didn't come out and you and Blue started acting all lovey-dovey."

"Nothing unusual," said Cory. "And how do you know Blue and I don't act lovey-dovey all the time when you're not there to see us?"

"You don't . . . I mean, I just . . . Never mind," Macks said, sounding even more confused.

After shouldering the knapsack with Weegie inside, Cory put on her sunglasses and helmet. They had scarcely started down the road when she had a strong vision of her mother beside a vision of Officer Deeds. At first visions like that had disturbed her. She'd even found them funny for a time. Now they made her wonder if she was doing something wrong by not making the match. "Only one more thing to worry about," she muttered to herself.

By the time they reached Micah's house, Weegie was squirming in the knapsack. Cory let her out and the woodchuck ran off to find Noodles. Cory didn't see their reunion, but she heard them squealing and a moment later the two were racing around the house.

"I guess she's feeling better," said Macks.

Cory knew precisely what she needed to do next. As soon as she stepped into the house, she wrote a message to her grandfather and placed it in the basket. A few minutes later the reply came; he would love to see her the next day.

Cory started cleaning again. This time she took down the curtains, washed them, hung them out to dry; swept the floors; and cleaned off the mantel under the nest of the finch that told the time. She was tidying up her bedroom when she realized that Blue would be back soon, so she made a simple supper of sandwiches and sweet potato chips.

Micah wasn't home in time for supper. Cory wasn't sure if he was still with Quince or had gone to work, but she saved him a sandwich when she and Blue ate. She also wrote a note reminding him that she would be bringing Shimmer back with her, at least for the night. After Blue helped her bring in the curtains and hang them again, Cory grabbed the knapsack and they hurried to get on his cycle.

The weather was beautiful when Cory and Blue drove up the side of the mountain to Olot's cave. So many things were going on in her life that she really enjoyed the normalcy of rehearsals and was looking forward to losing herself in her music. On the way there, she almost forgot about her problem with Shimmer and wasn't reminded until she walked in the cave door and the baby dragon flew at her.

Cory caught Shimmer, laughing, and hugged her close.

"I'm sorry we can't keep her," said Chancy, "but she really needs to be able to fly outdoors. And there's her breath, too. I'm afraid that it makes me sick to my stomach. But then so many things do these days. Seeing you together like this makes me think that she really belongs with you. Is there any way she could live with you?"

Cory shrugged. "Not at Micah's house, but I may have to move soon. He has a new girlfriend."

"Really?" said Chancy as they walked down the hallway. "That's wonderful for him, but not so wonderful for you, I guess. Where will you go?"

"I'm still working on that," Cory told her. "Is everyone here yet?"

"Daisy is running late, so she's not here, but Cheeble just showed up and everyone else was early. I see Blue is already talking to Olot. I heard about the yeti. Olot and I haven't seen him. We asked the pigs and they haven't, either."

"If he's one of the guilds' Big Baddies, he's really just here because of me. Listen, I'd better get ready," Cory said as she set Shimmer down. "I'm in the mood for some serious drumming!"

After greeting her bandmates, Cory sat on her stool and began to warm up. The drumsticks felt right in her hands and drumming was a good way to work out some of her feelings. After Daisy finally showed up, apologizing for being late, the band played "Summer Heat." They practiced some of their old favorites next, focusing on songs that the ogres always liked.

When they were finished, Olot called for their attention. "I told you at last rehearsal that we have a number of ogres booking us for parties, but there's been a new development. Since then I've heard from some of our regular venues. Apparently, our popularity with the ogres has made Jack Horner and a few others want us back. They're planning to hire ogre security, so there shouldn't be any more incidents with the guilds while we perform."

"That's great news!" Skippy called out while his girlfriends clapped.

"Hear! Hear!" shouted Cheeble.

"We'll be playing at the Shady Nook tomorrow night," said Olot. "See you then!"

Daisy came over while Cory was covering her drums. "I have to tell you how much I like Jonas! He's so nice and a real gentleman, unlike some of the neo-trolls I've dated recently. We're going out again as soon as I have some free time. Thank you so much for setting us up! Now I know why people hire you as their matchmaker. I don't owe you for this, do I?"

Cory laughed. "You don't owe me anything. I just want you to date a decent person for a change."

"That's a relief!" Daisy said. "I was a little worried because I know you aren't cheap. See you tomorrow!"

Cory was still smiling as her friend went down the hallway. When Blue walked up, Cory hurried to finish with her drums. "I'll be ready in a minute," she finally said. "I just have to get Shimmer."

The little dragon had been sitting with Skippy's girlfriends, but when she saw Cory coming toward her, she scurried over, making happy chortling sounds. Cory scooped up the little dragon and tucked her in the knapsack so that only her head stuck out. "You won't fit in here much longer," Cory said. "This is almost too tight now."

This time Blue made Cory wait in the cave while he fetched the cycle. She started watching for trouble before they'd even started out and kept looking from side to side as they sped down the road. When she didn't see the yeti where they'd last encountered him, she began to think he might have gone back to where he came from. She was startled when they made the next turn and saw him standing in the middle of the road.

"Hold on!" Blue shouted as he turned the cycle to the side. They sped off the road onto the steeper grade, jerking and jolting down the uneven ground of the mountainside with the yeti roaring after them.

Cory clamped her arms around Blue, trying not to fall off each time the cycle threatened to tip over or dump them. When the little dragon started to squirm in the knapsack, Cory shouted, "No, Shimmer! Stay where you are!"

Instead, the dragon pulled herself free and took to the air. Cory didn't see what she did next, but she heard the beat of the dragon's wings as she flew off. Suddenly the yeti's roar turned into a loud, high screech and a prolonged howl. When Cory glanced over her shoulder, the yeti was no longer chasing them. Finally reaching the next loop of the road, Blue turned the cycle onto the smooth surface. Then Shimmer was there, circling overhead as they sped down the side of the mountain.

"What just happened?" Blue shouted over his shoulder.

"I don't know," Cory shouted back. "But I think Shimmer just taught the yeti that you don't mess with dragons!"

⇛→

Shimmer flew circles over Cory and Blue all the way back to Micah's house. The little dragon landed in Cory's arms when Blue finally parked the cycle. They were starting for the porch when Shimmer squawked and pulled away from Cory. She glanced at the porch and saw that the fairy light was out. Squinting, Cory could just make out a dark figure hunched over the doormat. It occurred to her that Micah might have come home late from seeing Quince and had dropped his keys. She was about to call out to Shimmer when the figure stood. Whoever he was, he was taller and thinner than Micah.

Cory was still watching when Shimmer flew onto the porch. Opening her mouth, the little dragon breathed flames at the mysterious figure. Light blossomed when his cloak caught on fire. He dropped something with a clang and ran, screaming, off the porch and across the lawn.

Blue ran after the stranger, but gave up after passing three houses. When he came back, Cory had joined Shimmer on the porch, where the little dragon was devouring the stinky fish that had spilled from the dropped bucket.

"So much for the evidence," Blue said as Shimmer flipped the last fish into the air and caught it, letting it go straight down her gullet.

"I'd rather have Shimmer around than any smelly old evidence," Cory said, giving the satisfied dragon a hug.

Blue laughed. "I don't think the judge would appreciate it if we brought either one into court."

CHAPTER

15

Cory had hoped to talk to Micah about moving out, but just as she went into the kitchen that morning, he rushed out the door, claiming that he had students coming in for extra help. Disappointed, she promised herself that she'd corner him that night and have the conversation then. She almost told Blue, but decided to wait until after it was settled with her grandfather and she and Blue had more time to talk.

Cory didn't tell Macks that she was moving, either, but when she announced that they were going to see her grandfather again, the ogre couldn't hide his excitement. "That putti chef is great! She told me she could make whatever I wanted. She made me fried chicken and it was even better than my Gamma's, and she's the best cook I know! I don't want to ask for a lot, but do you think Creampuff would make me a roast beef and mashed potato sandwich covered in gravy?"

Cory tried not to shudder when she said, "I don't know why not."

"And maybe some pickled pigs' feet," he added, his eyes glazing over.

When they reached Lionel's house, the putti seemed just as excited to see them. Macks remembered the way to the kitchen and hurried there while Orville escorted Cory to the terrace.

"I'll be right back with your breakfast," the putti told Cory, and toddled off to get it.

Cory took her usual seat across from her grandfather. "I'm delighted to see you, my dear," said Lionel. "I must ask, however, does something in particular bring you here, or did you just miss my smiling face?"

"Actually, I came to see you about your offer. Were you serious when you said you wanted me to come live here with you?"

"Indeed, I was," said Lionel. "And the offer still stands. Is there something I can do to entice you into choosing in my favor?"

"You said before that Blue is welcome to stay here while he watches over me. How do you feel about dragons?" Cory asked him.

"That depends. Are you talking about your pet dragon, Shimmer? Because if you are, I would have no problem if you brought her with you on the condition that you must let her go free in the Enchanted Forest should she become too big for you to handle."

"I can agree to that," said Cory. "I thought we could build her a den out on the lawn where she could live and we won't have to worry that she's going to burn the house down. We could make it look nice from the outside and use cinder blocks inside."

"That sounds like an excellent plan," said Lionel.

"I would like to bring the woodchucks, if you don't mind. They could live in the backyard as well."

Lionel nodded. "I expected you to bring them."

"There's one more thing," said Cory. "Do you think you could teach me more about being a Cupid? I'm sure there's lots that I have yet to learn."

"It would be my pleasure! May I ask what precipitated this sudden urge to move?"

"I made a match for Micah yesterday, so I need to move out. He hasn't asked me to or anything, but I think it's time."

"Then by all means, my doors are open to you," Lionel said, beaming. "When would you like to make this move?"

"Would tomorrow be too soon?" she asked. "Micah really doesn't want Shimmer in his house."

"The sooner the better! I'll have my putti come help you pack first thing in the morning."

"That won't be necessary," said Cory. "I don't have much to move."

"Even so," said Lionel. "They'd be so disappointed if we didn't ask them."

Cory and her grandfather ate a pleasant breakfast together. They didn't speak much, but Cory enjoyed looking out over the river at the back of the long, sloping lawn. She could see herself sitting there with her grandfather every morning for many years to come; the thought made her feel good inside.

After breakfast, Cory met Macks in the hall outside the kitchen. He didn't seem happy about leaving, but he cheered up when she said they'd be back the next day. Although she was tempted to tell him that she was going to move to her grandfather's house, she wanted to wait until she had told Micah and Blue.

She wished she had mentioned it to Blue that morning, even if he had been acting distracted. *I'll tell him this afternoon as soon as I see him*, she told herself.

They were on their way to Micah's house when Cory *saw* a vision of her mother. Officer Deeds's image was there, too, and it made Cory wonder if it would even be possible to ignore a match that she didn't want to make. They were both unhappy people. Maybe they'd be happier if they were together.

Even though the putti were coming to help her the next day, Cory wanted to pack most of her things herself. She took out the boxes she'd used when she moved to Micah's house and filled them first, leaving the rest of her possessions for the putti to pack.

After what had happened during their last performance at the Shady Nook, Cory was nervous about the night's show. She changed her clothes for the performance, but couldn't bring herself to start supper.

"I'd rather wait to eat after the show," she told Blue when he arrived. "My stomach is in knots and I really don't think I could eat now."

"I understand," said Blue. "I'll get cleaned up and be ready to go in a few minutes."

"There's something I wanted to tell you first," Cory said. "I didn't want to say anything until I was positive that it was going to happen, but I talked to my grandfather this morning and he's fine with it. Remember when he invited me to move in with him? I've decided to take him up on it. I'm moving into his house tomorrow."

"Oh!" Blue said, looking surprised.

"Now that Micah has found his true love, I can't stay here. If they're like all the other matches I've made, they'll want to get married and Quince will move in here and I'll have to move out anyway. I might as well do it now before it gets awkward and Micah has to ask me to go."

"I get that part," said Blue.

"Do you remember Grandfather saying that you and the ogres would be welcome there? He's letting me take Shimmer and the woodchucks, too. The putti are coming over tomorrow to help me move."

"It sounds as if you really do have everything arranged," Blue said with an edge to his voice.

"You don't look happy. Is something wrong?"

"I just wish you had told me sooner," said Blue. "You could have mentioned that you were thinking about it. This is a big step for you to keep to yourself. I thought we were close enough to share all our big decisions. It was your decision to make, obviously, but still . . ."

Cory slipped her arms around his neck. "You're right. I'm sorry I didn't tell you about it from the beginning. It is something we should have talked about. But I think it will work out really well. My grandfather's house is big, so there's plenty of room for us there, and he has an enormous backyard. He's already agreed that we can build a den for Shimmer. I thought about finding a place of my own, but I'd have to rent for a while and no one is going to want to rent to someone with a pet dragon."

"Huh," Blue grunted.

"I am sorry!" Cory said, and stood on her tiptoes to kiss him.

Although Blue's arms hung by his sides when the kiss started, by the time it was over he was holding her close. "I forgive you," he murmured into her hair. "Just don't do it again! From now on, we share all big decisions."

"Agreed!" said Cory.

"If that's settled, I really do need to get ready," Blue said, and kissed her one last time before letting her go.

"There's no hurry," Cory told him. "I want to talk to Micah before we leave. He should be home soon."

Cory waited by the front window, watching for Micah. When Blue came out of the bathing room, Micah still wasn't there. "I forgot to tell you, Macks is going with us," Blue told her. "I talked to him about it on my way in."

"That's fine," Cory said, not really paying attention.

"Jack Horner has hired half a dozen ogres to watch the restaurant," Blue continued. "Macks and I are going to sit near you. The others will be stationed around the restaurant, watching for anything suspicious. Macks thinks that's more than we need, but I'm not so sure. I just hope that it's enough."

"With so many ogres there, I can't imagine that anyone is going to try anything," said Cory. "Ogres can look very intimidating when they want to, present company included."

"Are you almost ready to go?" Blue asked her. "The show starts in less than an hour."

"Not quite yet," Cory said, glancing out the window again.

Although they waited until they absolutely had to leave, there was still no sign of Micah. Cory was disappointed, but there wasn't a thing she could do about it.

When they reached the Shady Nook, a sea of solar cycles waited for them in front of the restaurant. Most of the bikes bore the markings of the solar-cycle gang. After slipping in the back entrance, Cory peeked through the door at the crowd already taking their seats. "I don't think we'll have to worry about a shortage of ogres. It looks as if the entire gang is here."

"There is quite a crowd," Blue said. "And there are more at the door waiting to come in. Jack Horner said he wanted extra security, and you know I agree with him. We can't be any too cautious where your safety is concerned."

"That's very sweet," said Cory. "But I just hope they leave room for the non-ogre audience."

Cory and her bandmates went onstage and began to warm up soon after that. She noted that there were two ogres at the door and four stationed on the sidewalk out front. Blue had sent some to watch the back door as well. Cory doubted very much that the guilds were going to make any sort of move that night.

She could hear people talking to each other about the new song, "Summer Heat," before they even started playing it. When she beat out the tempo for the introduction to the song, she could sense the crowd's anticipation rising. They were so caught up in the song's tale of a hot summer's day that Cory could have sworn she saw people wiping perspiration from their faces. As the last note of the song faded away, no one moved or made a sound. Then they were on their feet, clapping, while the members of the band grinned at each other.

They played some old favorites after that, and the crowd rode the wave of music with them from one song to another. When the band finally took a break, everyone was exhausted. As the lights came up and waiters circulated through the audience, Cory and the other members of Zephyr made their way to the room in the back where they usually took their breaks. A crowd gathered by the door to congratulate them on their performances. Cory was working her way through the press of people when someone grabbed her sleeve.

"I need to talk to you, Cory," said a voice. She looked up to see her ex-boyfriend, Walker.

"But I don't want to talk to you," Cory said, and tried to move on.

"I care about you, Cory, and I hate to see you hurting yourself this way," Walker said, still holding on to her. "I've heard about the mess you're in and how the guilds are all mad at you because you betrayed them."

"Leave me alone, Walker," said Cory as she tried to shake his hand loose.

"You're ruining your reputation," Walker told her. "If you don't stop working against the guilds now, no one will ever want to be your boyfriend again."

"That's a load of troll trash and you know it," Cory said, finally shaking his hand off her arm.

"She's right," Blue said, coming up behind Walker. "It is a lot of trash, but then telling lies is what you're good at. And she doesn't need any more boyfriends. Cory has me."

"I don't need or want anyone else, ever," said Cory. When Blue pulled her into his arms, she didn't need any more encouragement. Their kiss was long enough that people around them began to clap and made Walker storm off in a huff.

"You know," Blue said when their kiss finally ended, "you are so much better off without Walker."

"I know," Cory told him. "Because now I have the perfect guy. And before you make a joke out of this and ask who he is, I'll tell you that I'm looking at him right now."

She raised her eyes so that she was gazing into his, and they both knew that she meant what she said.

CHAPTER
16

*G*ood morning!" Micah called out the next morning when Cory walked into the kitchen. "How are you on this beautiful day?"

Cory yawned and glanced out the window. The day was windy and overcast. Somehow she guessed that he wasn't talking about the weather. "I'm good," she said as she took her seat. "I was hoping I could talk to you today. Actually, I wanted to talk to you yesterday, but it never worked out."

Micah set down his mug of cider. "I have some wonderful news for you. I'm getting married! You're going to have an aunt!"

Cory was too tired to pretend excitement over something she already knew. The performance of the night before had been a huge success, and Jack Horner had already booked Zephyr for three more shows. She had stayed up late with Blue and a group of their friends, so had gotten very little sleep. She wished she could be more enthusiastic about Micah's news, but just didn't have it in her right then.

"Aren't you going to ask her name?" asked Micah.

"What's her name?" Cory asked, stifling another yawn. If she hadn't wanted to talk to her uncle this morning, she would have slept in instead of getting up extra early. Unfortunately, talking to him seemed really hard when she was so tired.

"She's Quince Brookfield," said Micah. "Weegie's chiropractor! I've never believed in love at first sight, but now I know that it can really happen!"

"That's wonderful," Cory said, trying to force more enthusiasm into her voice.

"Cory, why aren't you more surprised?" asked Micah. "You sound as if you knew this already. Wait a minute. You didn't have anything to do with this, did you? Did you do your Cupid thing to me and Quince? Is that why it happened so fast?"

Micah's voice had become increasingly suspicious. The look in his eyes was enough to snap Cory out of her stupor. Although she wished he hadn't guessed, she certainly wasn't going to lie to him.

"All I did was encourage something that you were

discovering for yourself," said Cory. "Quince is your true love. She is the one you are meant to spend your life with. I didn't make something happen that wasn't supposed to eventually. I just speeded it up a little."

Micah looked as if he didn't like what he was hearing, so Cory didn't mention that she had brought them together, or that if it hadn't been for her, they might never have met. Sometimes, a little less knowledge could be a good thing, if only he didn't guess that, too.

"And you know she's my true love because . . . ," said Micah.

"I *saw* her in a vision every time I *saw* you! It's what I do, Micah. It's what all Cupids do. We know when two people are right for each other, and we do what we can to make it happen. You can't be upset with me for that. I just handed you your very own happily-ever-after on a silver platter!"

"I suppose that's a good thing," said Micah.

"It's a very good thing," Cory said, wanting him to have the joy back in his voice that he'd had just a minute before. "Tell me, have you set a date?"

"We'd like to do it in two weeks if we can get everything worked out," said Micah.

"Ah," said Cory. "Then it might help to know that I'm moving out today. Grandfather has invited me to live with him."

"Really?" Micah said. "Were you going to move out even if I hadn't met Quince?"

"Your marriage is only part of the reason I'm moving," said Cory. "Grandfather is letting me keep Shimmer at his house. We're going to build her a den in the backyard."

"That's perfect!" Micah told her. "I've felt bad that she couldn't live here. What about the woodchucks? Are you taking them, too? Because they could stay here if they'd rather. I've gotten used to having them around."

"I haven't asked them yet. I'll tell them that they have a choice."

"I'm glad things are working out for you, Cory," said her uncle. "You deserve it!"

"And I'm glad that you've found your own true love!" Cory replied.

"I should get going," Micah said, standing up. "I want you to know that I am grateful and always will be. It's just that I always thought I'd have some say in who I fell in love with. I don't doubt it when you say that she's my true love, because in my heart I know she is, so I guess it doesn't really matter. Will you be here when I get home tonight?"

"I don't think so," Cory said. "I should have moved to Grandfather's by then. You and Quince will have to come over for supper as soon as we get settled."

Micah bent down to give her a quick kiss on the cheek before he left the kitchen. Cory could hear him going out the front door as she poured herself a bowl of mixed grains and milk. She looked up when the kitchen door opened.

"That didn't go too badly," Blue said as he sat down and reached for a bowl. He looked rumpled and still half asleep, but Cory thought he looked adorable.

"How much of the conversation did you hear?" Cory asked him.

"Most of it," said Blue. "I sleep on the floor of the main room about ten feet from this door. I'd have to be very determined to *not* hear conversations that take place in this kitchen. You told me yesterday that the putti are coming to help you move. I've never met any putti, but I understand they look like babies. I can't imagine that they'll be much help."

"It should be interesting," Cory admitted. "I can't wait to see it myself."

After a quick breakfast, Blue changed his clothes and left for work. Once he was gone, Cory got dressed while Macks sat on the porch and kept an eye on Shimmer. Cory was on her way to ask Macks if he would like a cup of cider when the message basket *pinged!* She was surprised to see that the message was from Blue.

Cory,

I'm sending more ogres to watch over you today. After some unexpected testimony from an elderly tooth fairy, the guilds are starting to worry. Some new nasty threats have been uncovered and most of them were aimed at you. I am afraid that they hope to disrupt the trial and frighten off the last few witnesses by doing something to you. Your new ogre bodyguards should arrive within the hour.

Love,
Blue

"I wonder what the guilds are planning now?" Cory muttered. She glanced out the window, half expecting to see something awful, but everything looked the way it usually did. She shook her head at her own foolishness. Whatever they were planning, it was bound to happen when she didn't expect it.

Cory showed the message to Macks, then had to go back inside when she heard the basket *ping!* again. The next message was from her grandfather, saying that the putti were on their way. Cory went outside to look for the woodchucks. She found Noodles and Weegie in the garden, nibbling dandelion leaves.

"I need to talk to you," she said, and sat down by the edge of the garden. "I'm moving to my grandfather Lionel's house today."

"We figured something was up when we saw you stuck half your stuff in boxes," said Weegie. "Noodles said that the last time you put your stuff in boxes, you brought him here."

"That's true," Cory told her. "I just wanted to tell you that you're both invited to go with me. My grandfather has a big yard that leads down to the river. It's really pretty and I think you'd like it. If you don't want to go with me, you could either move to the park across the street or stay here with Micah. He's already said that he'd like to have you stay."

Weegie turned to Noodles and grumbled. Cory waited while they grumbled, twitched their ears, and nudged each other. Finally, Weegie turned back to her and said, "Can we go with you to check out the place? If we don't like it, we'll want you to bring us back here."

Cory nodded. "We can do that. We'll be leaving in a little while, so don't go far."

She was starting to stand up when Shimmer made a chirping sound and landed beside her. The little dragon tried to climb in her lap, and protested when Cory set her back on the ground. "Sorry, sweet girl, but I need to finish getting ready. My helpers should be here soon."

Cory was about to go in the house when Wanita called from the walkway, "Cory, I see you have your friend back. Is your uncle letting you keep her this time?"

"Hi, Wanita," said Cory as the little witch struggled to drag Boris away from the newly planted shrubs. "Actually, we're both leaving. I'm moving in with my grandfather and Shimmer is going with me."

"That's too bad!" Wanita told her. "The part about you leaving, I mean. We'll miss you in the neighborhood. Oh, before I forget, I wanted to tell you my news. I heard that the guilds are using a lot of pressure to get Witches United to join them. Rumor says that the guilds in the alliance don't think they have a chance without all the power that the witches can bring, and because Organized Witches of the World is a bunch of pansy-faced, goody-two-shoes witches, they want the members of WU. Since no one knows which way the WU brooms will fly, the trial is still up in the air, so to speak. Say, I have to go. My bridge club is coming over today. We're going to decide which bridge to destroy this week. Good luck with your move and keep in touch!"

As Cory watched Wanita half walk, half drag her pet boar down the street, it occurred to her how much she was going to miss Micah's neighbors. She could invite them to parties and see them around town, but it wouldn't be the same.

The whisper of a solar vehicle made Cory turn and look in the other direction. A large solar cart used to haul big items was coming down the road. Three putti sat on the driver's seat that usually held one person. Cory recognized Orville and two of the other putti she'd seen at her grandfather's house. She smiled and waved as she walked to the curb to wait for them.

Orville jumped off the solar cart first. "We're so excited that you're moving in with us! We'll take care of the move. All you need to do is show us what you want to take and we'll get started."

"Right this way," Cory said, and led them to the porch. They passed Macks, who was tossing a ball into the air for Shimmer to catch. The little dragon swooped over the putti, making them cry out in surprise.

"Hey, Orville!" Macks said when he saw the putti. "Don't worry. Shimmer won't hurt you! This little girl only goes after the people who pester Cory."

Eyes wide, Orville turned from Shimmer to Cory. "You have a dragon?"

Cory nodded. "She's moving with me. Grandfather gave his approval." She began to wonder if taking Shimmer was going to be a problem. It would never work out if the putti were afraid of her.

"We're going to have a dragon at the house!" Orville shrieked. "That's wonderful! Wait till everyone hears about this!"

Cory grinned as the putti began to jump up and down. Apparently, they weren't afraid after all.

"Uh, Cory, did I hear you say something about moving?" asked Macks.

Cory gave herself a mental kick. She had told everyone except Macks. "I'm sorry! I forgot to tell you. I'm moving to my grandfather's house today."

Macks's grin was so wide that Cory thought his face might split in two. "That's great! Nothing against your uncle's house, but it is kind of small for all of us. Say, this means I'll get to eat that great food every day! Not that you aren't a good cook, but no one can beat Creampuff!"

"It's all right, Macks. I know how much you like her cooking. Orville and I are going to finish packing my things. Please keep an eye on Shimmer, and watch for the other ogres Blue sent over. They should be here soon."

Taking the putti inside, she set them to work packing the last of her possessions while she collected her toothbrush and a few other things she'd kept in the bathing room. When she came out, Macks had come to tell her that the other ogres had arrived and would be happy to help her move. With the ogres carrying the boxes out and the putti straightening her bedroom, Cory was soon ready to leave.

After checking the house one last time and locking the door behind her, Cory headed toward Macks's solar cycle. Orville met her on the way. "The female woodchuck tells us that she and her mate are going as well. We brought extra boxes and they chose one to ride in. They are already on the solar cart. Are you ready to go?"

"As soon as I get my dragon," Cory told him.

Shimmer had picked up on the excitement of the move and was hard to catch, but eventually Cory was able to coax her down with the sight of her favorite ball. With the little dragon tucked in the knapsack, they finally started out. Two ogres rode their solar cycles first, with Cory and Macks right behind them. The solar cart came next with the other ogres following. People stopped and stared as they rode past. "I'm sure the guilds will know that I've moved after this," Cory told Macks. "I hope they leave Micah alone now."

It didn't take long to drive to Lionel's house. The ogres seemed very impressed as they parked their solar cycles in the driveway and started carrying the boxes inside. Cory had Macks carry the box holding the woodchucks around back before he set it down. Weegie and Noodles ambled out of the box, sniffed the air, and took off into the yard. Impatient, Shimmer wiggled out of the knapsack while Cory was still wearing it. The little dragon leaped into the air, leaving Cory to watch her circle over the yard and head to the river.

"Should I call her back?" asked Macks.

Cory shook her head. "She'll come back when she's ready. I want to go say hello to my grandfather and pick out a bedroom so the putti can unpack."

Lionel was in his study thumbing through a binder filled with leaves, so his greeting was brief. He did tell her where to look for a bedroom, however, promising to meet her for lunch. Although Cory had a seemingly endless number of rooms to choose from, it didn't take her long to make her decision. She picked a room that looked out over the back lawn and gave her a clear view of the river. There was a small balcony off the room, providing the perfect place for a baby dragon to land.

When Cory returned downstairs, she found that the putti had set tables on the lawn and were carrying out a feast fit for dozens of ogres. Although Cory knew how much Macks liked the chef, she wasn't sure how the rest of the ogres would get along with the putti. Her concerns vanished when she saw one of the ogres carrying five putti at once while the little men laughingly asked him to put them down. She was impressed with how gentle the big ogres were around the babylike people and how thrilled the putti seemed to be to have the ogres there.

"Maybe I should have done this sooner," she said to herself.

Cory was watching the festive scene when she saw Shimmer fly over the yard and head around the house to the front. Worried that the dragon might startle a neighbor or fly into an oncoming solar cycle, Cory hurried around the side of the house. She stopped in the curve of the driveway, unsure where to look next. Her hands were already cupped around her mouth, ready to call to Shimmer, when she heard someone talking.

"Aren't you the cutest thing! Where did you come from, young lady? You don't act wild. Do you belong to one of my neighbors?"

Cory followed the voice across the side lawn and through a grouping of trees. There she found an elderly, silver-haired woman petting the baby dragon.

"You found Shimmer!" Cory said. The little dragon scurried across the ground to Cory, who bent down to scoop her up.

"She belongs to you?" the woman asked in disbelief. "She's a beautiful creature. Where did you purchase her?"

"I didn't buy her," Cory said, and laughed when the baby dragon licked her, leaving a hot trail down her cheek. "She was given to me and I was thrilled to get her."

"As well you should be," said the woman. "Who are you, girl? Haven't I met you before?"

"I'm Cory Feathering. Lionel Feathering is my grandfather. I just moved in, so I guess I'm your new neighbor."

"Ah, yes. I saw you at the trial. You've gotten quite a reputation these past few weeks. I wonder how much of it is true. Tell me, what do you plan to do with a baby dragon?"

Cory was a little baffled by the change in topic. "I, uh, intend to take good care of her while she grows up. I already promised my grandfather that I'd let her go if she got too big for me to handle."

"Uh-huh," said the woman. "We'll see if you really do. I understand that you're no longer a tooth fairy. So what is it you do now, or are you too good to work?"

Cory didn't like the way the woman was talking to her, but she didn't want to offend one of her grandfather's neighbors on the day she moved in. "I've started a matchmaking business and I'm in a band," Cory told her.

The woman gave her a long look up and down. "That's right, you're a matchmaker. Did you go to a trade school for that?"

"I don't believe there are any classes for it," said Cory. The woman was making her feel oddly uncomfortable. Cory started to edge away.

"And yet you claim to know how to do it? How is that possible?"

"Just a knack, I suppose," Cory said. "I need to go. I'm glad Shimmer wasn't bothering you. Good-bye! It was nice meeting you."

As Cory hurried back to her grandfather's yard, she thought about the silver-haired woman. She had asked a lot of questions, but Cory hadn't learned a thing about her.

Cory found Macks seated at one of the tables and handed Shimmer to him. "Would you please keep an eye on her? Try not to let her go out front."

"It'll be my pleasure," said Macks. "Shimmer, let's see if we can find your ball. I bet none of these galoots have ever seen a dragon catch a ball before."

While Macks took care of Shimmer, Cory went looking for her grandfather in his study. He was putting away the binder when she knocked on his door. "I just met one of your neighbors," Cory told him. "She's an older woman with silver hair and she seems awfully nosy. All she did was ask me questions."

"That would be Laudine Kundry. She's lived next door to me for sixty-five years. You may not have heard of her, but she's the head of the guild called Witches United."

"She's the head of WU?" said Cory. "Well, that's just great. The woman obviously doesn't like me, and I've heard that the other guilds are pressuring WU to join their alliance against guild reform. This will probably push her over to their side."

"That isn't good," her grandfather said. "WU is made up of the nastier, more powerful witches. The guilds probably think that with WU on their side, people will be afraid to speak out against their alliance. Is it possible that you misread her? She really hasn't had time to form an opinion of you yet."

"I may not know her, but I do know when someone doesn't like me," said Cory. "And that woman doesn't like me one little bit."

CHAPTER
17

Cory woke early the next day and wanted to hurry downstairs, but she had things to do first. Her grandfather's house didn't seem like the kind of place where she could wear her nightgown and robe to breakfast or show up without brushing her hair. She dressed and washed up as quickly as she could before making her way to the terrace.

Her grandfather was reading *The Fey Express* while he waited for her. He smiled when he looked up and said, "You can't imagine how happy I am that you moved in, my dear. This old house has been too quiet for too long. You've been here less than a day, but you've already breathed new life into the place. And I haven't seen the putti this happy in decades! Would you believe I heard Orville singing this morning? He has a very nice baritone. Tell me, do you have any plans for today?"

Cory nodded. "The ogres offered to build the den in the backyard for Shimmer. Would you be able to look at the yard and help us decide where we should place it?"

"Of course! I have to tell you that I strolled down to the river this morning as I do every day. I saw your two woodchucks. They've been digging a den for themselves near the trees. One of them actually spoke to me!"

"That would be Weegie," said Cory. "She's Noodles's mate."

"Ah," said Lionel. "She told me that they like it here and want to stay. She asked me to tell you that it's much better than the park."

"I thought they'd like it here," Cory told him.

"Ah, good, here's Blue," Lionel said. "Orville and Margory should be along with breakfast shortly. I believe your ogre friends have already started their breakfast in the kitchen."

"I'm afraid I have to eat and run," Blue said as he sat down at the table. He took a sip of the berry juice that was already beside his plate. "The trial is almost over and I'll be spending my day in the courtroom."

"It must be exciting at this point," said Cory.

"Not too exciting, I hope," Blue replied. "Excitement

in a fey courtroom often means that someone is up to something bad. That's why we always have at least three witches sitting in during a big trial to make sure nothing gets out of hand. Of course, that might work against us if WU joins the guild alliance. I don't know what we'd do then."

"I remember years ago when an ogre dragged his neighbor to court over a pet basilisk," said Lionel.

Cory would have liked to have heard the story, but just then Shimmer flew past, heading to the front of the house. "Excuse me," Cory said, getting to her feet. "I have to go after Shimmer. I'll be right back."

The little dragon was nowhere to be seen when Cory reached the front yard. Cory called, "Shimmer!" but the dragon didn't come. She walked around the yard calling, yet there was no rustle in the underbrush or little head peeking out from behind the fountain to chirrup hello. Thinking that the dragon might have gone to visit Laudine Kundry again, Cory walked through the trees and up to the front door.

Although there was no bell like Lionel's on the door, there was a circular door knocker with a strange shape in the middle. Cory picked it up and let it fall. A whisper of sound came from inside the house. A moment later, Laudine opened the door.

"You've come looking for your dragon," she said without a greeting. "I've given her some fresh fish. Come inside while she finishes eating."

Cory thought this was odd for two reasons. First, why would anyone bring someone else's pet into her house to feed it when it lives next door? And second, why would Cory have to wait for Shimmer to eat? The little dragon could devour a tub of fish in a few quick gulps. Cory didn't mention either of these points, however. This was her grandfather's neighbor and the head of a powerful guild that she hoped wouldn't turn against her. Antagonizing Laudine Kundry at this point would be a very bad idea.

Instead, Cory followed the woman into her house and took a quick look around as they started down a long hall. The hall led from a small foyer to a closed door at the back of the house. Other doors opened off on either side. Although most of them were closed, a few were open to bright sunny rooms filled with antiques. Pictures of somber-looking people decorated the walls of the hallway, while a soft, colorful carpet stretched down the center of the floor, muffling their footsteps as they walked.

Laudine finally stopped at the second to last door. "This way," she said, and gestured Cory inside.

Cory walked a few feet and stopped to look around. They were in a very odd room, with no little dragon, no windows, and no furniture. Suddenly uneasy, she turned to say something to Laudine, who was already shutting the door.

"Now we'll see what you really are!" said Laudine. "I've been asking around about you. I know you've been hiding something, and I'm going to find out what it is!"

"What are you talking about?" Cory asked her. The lights went out, leaving Cory and Laudine in the absolute dark. "Are you having problems with your lights? I can call a fairy workman to come out for you. It's a weekday, so he shouldn't charge you an emergency fee."

Laudine didn't say anything as the temperature in the room dropped. A cold wind rushed past Cory, lifting her hair and chilling her skin. Fear trickled through her like water dripping from an icicle.

"Show yourself!" Laudine barked.

"I'm standing right here!" Cory exclaimed. "If your lights were working, you'd see me plain as day. What in the name of all things growing are you doing?"

Laudine began to chant something in a language Cory didn't understand. Cory staggered as the wind buffeted her, pushing at her from all different directions.

She gasped when something started spinning her around. Cory's stomach lurched and her heart began to pound painfully fast. For the first time she felt as if she was in real danger.

Images of Cory started to flash on the walls as she spun faster and faster. She saw herself as a child, playing in her mother's garden with Daisy, then later, collecting a tooth from under a little boy's pillow. Pressure built up around her, squeezing her so that it was hard to breathe. The image of Cory standing inside the glass tube as the Tooth Fairy Guild stripped away her fairy abilities flashed past. For a moment there was nothing, then an image of her shuffling out of the tube, weak and sickly looking. Again there was nothing but the dark space around her, then an image of Cory playing the drums at the Shady Nook appeared. This time when the blackness took over, the pressure around her began to build until it hurt. Laudine's chanting grew louder and louder, making Cory's head ache until the pressure inside her was as great as the pressure around her.

Finally, Cory couldn't take it anymore. She hadn't wanted to show her Cupid side, but there was no need to die to keep the secret. "Enough!" she cried, and thought, *Wings!*

Cory's wings were there an instant later, iridescent in the dark. She stopped spinning as her wings opened.

The pressure disappeared, yet the fear and unease lingered. Cory closed her eyes and thought about love, just as she had when banishing the effect of the worry monster from the house. She thought about Blue and how she'd felt at the Shady Nook when he kissed her, about her grandfather and the look on his face when she came down for breakfast that very morning, and about the joy on the faces of the putti and the ogres when they played together on the lawn. When she thought about the way Micah and Quince had looked together after she'd shot them with her arrows, she was no longer afraid.

Cory opened her eyes to find that the room was lit with a rosy glow emanating from her. The witch was standing in front of her, her eyes huge as she gazed at Cory, who was suspended six feet above the floor with nothing holding her up and no effort on her part. Even after Cory settled to the floor, the glow remained.

"You're a demigod!" Laudine declared, her voice hoarse from chanting.

Cory realized that she was clutching her bow in one hand and her quiver in the other.

"Are you a Cupid?" asked the witch.

Cory sighed and nodded. There was no use denying it now. She sent the bow and quiver away with a thought.

"I've heard of Cupids, but I never knew they were real!" said Laudine. "I became suspicious after you made time stand still in the courtroom. I didn't see what you did; I just thought you must be an undeclared witch who had cast an unauthorized love spell, violating all the witchly codes. I never dreamed that you were a Cupid and the love you brought was the real thing! I am so sorry! If I'd had a clue, I never would have put you through this! Oh, my! What must you think of me? And your grandfather . . . Is he a Cupid as well? I ask only because I met my late husband through him. That man was the love of my life, but I never would have met him if your grandfather hadn't introduced us. We were married a few weeks later. I've always said that the way we met was magical, but I had no idea it really was! Why do you two keep it a secret? The guilds would lose their case immediately if everyone knew who you are."

"Because letting everyone know would make our jobs harder. Cupids need to work without anyone being aware of what they're doing," said Cory.

Laudine was shaking when she held up her hand. "I won't tell a soul about either of you. I promise!"

Cory nodded and something she'd never felt before came over her. When she spoke, her voice didn't sound quite like her own. "I accept your solemn promise and will hold you to it for as long as love exists."

The glow that still surrounded Cory seemed to engulf Laudine so that it embraced them both. And then it was gone, leaving them in the dark again. When the lights came back on, Cory glanced at her wings and thought them away.

"Let me take you to your dragon," Laudine said as she opened the door.

Cory followed her out of the room and down the hall. She could hear something scratching at one of the doors, so wasn't surprised when the witch opened it and Shimmer came bounding out, running straight to Cory.

"I must apologize again," said Laudine, her cheeks flaming. "I'm so embarrassed that I did this!"

"I forgive you," Cory said as she bent to pick up Shimmer. "But let's not do it again. Ever!"

CHAPTER
18

As Laudine's door closed behind her, Cory turned her face to the sun and hugged Shimmer. Although the warmth of Cory's glow had chased the chill from her body, she still shivered when she thought about what had just happened.

Hearing sounds from the back of her grandfather's house, Cory made her way through the trees and across the wide lawn. She could hear ogres shouting and laughing before she'd even walked around the house. When she reached the corner, she spotted the ogres down by the river. Her grandfather was with them, talking to Macks.

Shimmer squirmed in Cory's arms, wanting to get down. When Cory set her on the ground, the little dragon flapped her wings and flew to Macks. Cory hurried after her. As she drew closer, she spotted dirt flying out of the ground, landing in an ever-growing pile. "They must have started Shimmer's den already," Cory murmured.

Lionel turned at Cory's approach and smiled. "There you are! I thought you and Shimmer had gotten lost. The putti have been looking for you. I was thinking about calling the FLEA."

"About that," Cory began. She wanted to tell him about what had happened with Laudine, but thought better of it when she saw the interested look on Macks's face. "I'll tell you later. So, what did you decide to do about the den for Shimmer?"

"That's what we've been discussing. The den is going to be mostly underground with an opening facing the river."

"And it's going to be big enough for a full-grown dragon, even though baby girl here is just itsy bitsy now, aren't you, Shimmer?" said Macks as he petted the baby dragon. "A couple of the guys have gone to get the material we need and the rest are digging the hole."

"What are you doing?" Cory asked.

"I'm supervising!" said Macks. "It's a tough job, but somebody's got to do it."

An ogre wearing his hair in a stringy ponytail walked up to Macks. "The guys are back from Cave and

Den Warehouse. They want to know where they should dump the stone."

"Excuse me," Macks told Cory and Lionel. "A supervisor's job is never done."

As the ogres walked away, Cory turned to her grandfather. "I wanted to tell you that I saw Laudine this morning. She knows about us."

"You mean that we're . . ."

"Cupids," Cory said, nodding. "It couldn't be helped. I didn't know that witches could do the things she did. She promised not to tell anyone about us, though. I have a feeling that it was a binding vow."

"Learned about that, did you?" said Lionel. "It was going to happen sooner or later. Those vows really can't be broken. As for Laudine, I suppose I should have expected this. She's a powerful woman who is used to getting what she wants. If she was curious about you, she was going to find out the truth one way or another."

The ogres were driving the solar cart loaded with large rocks and bags of cement down the length of the lawn. Cory and her grandfather watched them park the cart and begin to unload beside the hole in the ground. A procession of putti carrying tables and baskets of food came out of the house next. Seeing them, the ogres cheered and began to work faster.

"That must be lunch," said Lionel. "The ogres love to eat and the putti love to feed them. Creampuff is delighted to cook for people who truly enjoy the food she prepares. I've been a great disappointment to her lately. My appetite just isn't what it used to be. But now! Let's just say that your friends are very welcome here."

"How long was I gone?" Cory asked. "When I left to look for Shimmer, we were just about to eat breakfast. It felt like I wasn't gone for long, but you've already accomplished so much, and now the putti are serving lunch!"

"You were gone for hours, my dear! One of these days you'll have to tell me exactly what transpired in Laudine's house. Ah, here comes Orville. It looks as if he has a message for you."

"This just arrived, miss," Orville said, presenting a silver tray bearing a folded message.

"Who is it from, Orville?" Cory asked as she reached for it.

"I have no idea, miss," Orville said stiffly. "I never read a Cupid's personal messages."

Watching the putti's retreating back, Cory said to her grandfather, "I hope I didn't insult him. I was just curious."

"He wasn't insulted. He's probably happy that he had a reason to let you know that he'll never read your messages. He doesn't read mine either, but I think he reads everyone else's. What does the message say?"

Cory had already opened it and was surprised to see that it was from Wanita. She read the message out loud to her grandfather.

Cory,

I just got word that WU has declared it is not joining the alliance against you. I thought you would want to know.

Your friend,

Wanita

"That's fantastic!" Cory said, gazing at the message in disbelief. She read it over again, just to make sure she hadn't misread something.

"I guess knowing who you really are made a difference to Laudine," said Lionel.

"She said that I should tell everyone. She thinks that the guilds wouldn't stand a chance in the trial if everyone knew who I was."

"In that case, I'm even happier that she made a solemn vow not to tell anyone," Lionel declared. "However, Laudine's knowing may just turn the tide. Losing WU as a possible ally will be a major blow against the power the other guilds can wield. Now, look at this. It appears we have some visitors."

Cory followed her grandfather's gaze to two people walking across the lawn. She was delighted when she realized that they were Serelia and Rina. "Hello!" she called as she hurried to greet them. "What are you doing back so soon?"

"We got word that Rina's mother had her baby," said Serelia. "It's a healthy boy."

"My parents haven't picked a name for him yet," Rina chimed in. "I think they should call him River, but they like Omar or Fred. I got to hold him today. He's so cute!"

"Cute as a button," Serelia said, looking as excited and happy as Rina. "We came back with Gladys and her children. They didn't get along with Rupert's mother. No surprise there. Hardly anyone gets along with Queen Aleris. Anyway, we asked around and heard that you had moved here, so we came to say hello."

"I'm glad you did! Come here, I want you to meet someone special. Grandfather, this is Serelia Quirt. She's Head Water Nymph at Misty Falls. And this is Rina Diver, Serelia's new apprentice. Serelia, Rina, this is my grandfather Lionel Feathering."

"It's a pleasure to meet you, ladies," said Lionel. "I'm

afraid you caught us on a rather busy day. Cory's ogre friends are building a den for her baby dragon."

"A baby dragon! Can I see it?" Rina asked.

"Go right ahead," said Cory. "She's with Macks, the ogre in the green shirt."

Serelia smiled indulgently as Rina took off running. "She's a delightful child," said the water nymph. "I'm so glad her parents gave me the opportunity to train her. She's a quick learner and very bright. Rina has already thought of some new ways of doing things that had never occurred to me."

"I'm so glad it's working out," Cory told her. "Listen, why don't you stay for a while? There's plenty of food and I'm sure Shimmer would love to play with Rina. The putti have set up tables under the trees and it's such a beautiful day."

"I think we will!" said Serelia. "I'll go tell Rina. She'll love it!"

"Serelia Quirt!" said Lionel when he and Cory were alone again. "I've heard of her, but I've never actually met her before. She's very influential in the water nymph world."

"And she's a very nice person," Cory told him. "I really think that—"

"Excuse me," her grandfather said in a lowered voice, "but it looks as if we have more company. Here comes

Laudine. She hasn't come over since your grandmother was here."

Cory turned around. Laudine was striding purposefully across the lawn, headed in their direction.

"Hello, Laudine," Lionel called. "How good of you to stop by."

"Hello, Lionel. It's been a long time," said Laudine. "I just came by to tell your granddaughter that WU will not be joining the alliance. I never did feel comfortable joining ranks with either Mary Mary or Flora Petalsby. They're a pair of ninnies as far as I'm concerned. 'Treat your guild members right and they'll be loyal forever' is what I always say. WU has never mistreated a member and never will. It's disgraceful what those two women have had done to fairies who once belonged to their guilds. That's all I wanted to say, so I'll leave you to your party."

"It isn't a party, or at least it didn't start out as one," said Cory. "Would you like to stay for lunch? Serelia Quirt and her new apprentice just stopped by. You might enjoy meeting them."

"Actually, I think I would!" said Laudine. "I've heard of Serelia, but I've never met her. I've never been to Misty Falls, for that matter." Without waiting for an introduction, Laudine left Cory and Lionel and walked up to Serelia on her own.

The two women were soon talking and seemed to be enjoying themselves. Cory didn't want to interrupt them, so she said to her grandfather, "We might as well eat now, too. I see the putti have set up chairs by the river. We can serve ourselves and go there to eat."

"That sounds very nice," said her grandfather. "Ladies first!"

By the time Cory and Lionel got in line, Serelia, Rina, and Laudine had already gotten their food and carried it to the chairs by the river. Cory helped herself to a sampling of salads while her grandfather took a few spoonfuls of different things. Lionel and Cory found seats near their guests and began to eat. Rina started chattering about Shimmer, who was asleep at her feet, and Cory sat back to enjoy her friend's company.

They hadn't been sitting there long when Rina pointed at the water. "Look at all the fish!" she exclaimed.

"That's odd," said Serelia as she squinted at the river. "It's not a normal school. There are all different kinds of fish swimming together."

"I've never seen that before," Laudine told her. "Strange."

Macks had come over at the first mention of fish. "I should go get a net! Hey, Alecks, do you have a net with you? You wouldn't believe the fish over here."

The ogres came running, some still carrying their plates.

Lionel leaned forward, nearly dumping his food on the ground. "What is that shape coming up through the water?"

"Whatever it is, it's huge and it's coming fast," said Cory.

Suddenly, a reddish-brown shape erupted from the water, sending waves over the bank and the feet of the assembled party. Shimmer was washed into Rina's legs and woke up, flapping her wings and hissing.

Instead of sinking back, the shape floated on the surface like an island, taking up most of the river's width. When Cory saw two eyes as big as dinner plates staring at them, she shouted, "Get back, Rina!" and reached for the child. Macks was faster, however. Plucking Rina from her seat, he handed her to one of his friends, who carried her farther inland with Shimmer following them, crying.

Orville was running as fast as his babylike legs could carry him toward Lionel, calling out, "I'm coming, sir!" when two enormously long tentacles stretched out in front of the monster, reaching for Cory and her grandfather. Eight not-quite-as-long arms waved above the water, waiting to receive their victims.

"It's a kraken!" shouted Macks.

When Cory saw her grandfather stand, she jumped up and knocked her chair out of the way, clearing a path for him to leave. She had started to pull him back when she glanced at the kraken and saw that there wasn't time; the tentacles were only feet away. And then the ogres were there, throwing themselves on the tentacles, squeezing them with their powerful arms and stabbing them with whatever they had in hand—a knife one had been using to cut his meat, a soup spoon, a trowel from the back of the solar cart.

While the ogres fought the tentacles, Cory tried to get her grandfather away from the water. Orville finally reached them and began tugging on the old man's hand, trying to lead him to safety. It wasn't until Lionel was behind the row of fallen chairs, on his way up the lawn, that Cory noticed Serelia. The water nymph was standing at the river's edge, holding her arms over the water. As the river began to roil closest to where she stood, the kraken's gaze shifted toward her. The disturbance in the water grew until it was pushing against the kraken, shoving it farther from the shore. Flailing its arms, the kraken fought against Serelia's current, trying to stay by the riverbank. Then Rina was back and water pounded on the kraken's bulbous head. The kraken rolled under the surface and came back up, closer than before.

The two water nymphs worked together then, beating at the kraken and trying to shove it away with the very water that supported it. "Maybe I can help," said Laudine. Chanting something under her breath, she made intricate motions with her hands. A moment later, the kraken's arms tied themselves in knots and the monster sank from sight.

Still working together, Serelia and Rina created a surge of water that carried the kraken downstream. Cory could see it just below the surface as it rushed past, struggling to free itself from the knots and the current. The water nymphs stayed by the river's bank long after the kraken was out of sight.

"What are they doing?" Macks asked Cory as the other ogres helped the putti pick up the chairs and clean up the debris left by the kraken's attack.

"I can answer that," said Laudine. "They're pushing the kraken downriver and out to sea. It's a long way, so they'll be at it for a good long time. While they do that, I'm going to register a formal complaint with the Itinerant Troublemakers Guild, file charges with the FLEA, and call a meeting of my guild. I don't know if the allied guilds did this because I refused to join them and it was a last act of desperation, or if they'd already had this attack planned. Whatever the reason, it was the wrong thing to do. These guilds aren't going to get away with this. They just bought themselves a whole cauldron full of trouble that I'm sure they weren't expecting."

While Laudine strode off, her jaw set in a grim line, Cory went looking for Shimmer. The little dragon was huddled under a table, shaking, as three putti tried to coax her out. As soon as she saw Cory, Shimmer launched herself at her, making frightened mewling sounds. Cory carried her up the lawn to the terrace, where she settled into her chair.

Shimmer had pressed her face into the crook of Cory's arm when Cory began to sing softly to her. She was stroking the baby dragon's back when Orville toddled up and said, "May I get you something, miss?"

"Just tell me how my grandfather is doing, please," Cory told him.

"He's fine. I took him to his room so he can rest. That was a lot more excitement than he's used to here."

"I don't think anyone could ever be used to that much excitement," Cory said with a laugh. "Please let me know if he needs me."

"I will, miss," Orville said, and went back inside the house.

Cory was still holding Shimmer on her lap when Serelia and Rina joined her. "I'm going to call for an emergency meeting of the Water Nymph Guild," Serelia told her. "As past president, I still have a lot of pull. People are going to answer for this."

"Thank you both for all that you did," said Cory. "I don't know what would have happened if you and Laudine hadn't been here."

"It was fun!" Rina declared. "Let me know if I can help out again!"

"I hope that's the last time I need that kind of help," said Cory. "But thank you for offering!"

It was very quiet after Serelia and Rina left. The ogres had gone inside to change out of their wet clothes, and the putti had finished carrying all the food and dishes, chairs, tables, and trash inside. Cory was still sitting on the terrace with Shimmer when Blue walked up.

He bent down to hug her, earning a squawk of protest from Shimmer. "I heard about what happened," he said, cupping Cory's chin in his hand as he looked into her eyes. "Are you all right?"

"I'm fine. We all are," said Cory. "But I'm afraid that there isn't any evidence for you to collect this time."

"I think I've got it covered," said Blue. "I have enough witness reports right here to convince any jury." He tapped his leaf pad and set it on the table. "And from what I hear, certain guilds are going to be facing a whole new set of lawsuits if Serelia Quirt and Laudine Kundry have anything to say about it."

"Which they will," said Cory.

"Oh, I'm sure you're right," Blue told her. "I have some news for you, too. The trial is just about over. They gave their concluding arguments today. Now all that's left is for the jury to deliberate. I doubt it's going to take them very long."

"I'd like to be there when they announce their decision," said Cory.

Blue chuckled. "I'm sure a lot of people want to be there, but you'll definitely have a seat. Tomorrow should be a very interesting day."

CHAPTER
19

The courtroom was already crowded when Cory took her seat between Lionel and Macks. She spotted Stella Nimble sitting with Jack and Marjorie a few rows away. Laudine was in the next row with Serelia. Delphinium was sitting behind Mary Mary, who kept turning around to talk to her.

"Who is that seated beside Flora Petalsby?" Cory asked her grandfather.

"That's Torsha Potts," said Lionel. "She's been head of the Frost Fairy Guild for a few months now. The brownie beside her is Twyven Deen, head of the House-cleaning Guild. I was surprised when he allowed his guild to ally themselves with Mary Mary and Flora Petalsby. He's usually very levelheaded. The man with gray hair is Kile Sleepwell, head of the Sandman

Guild. I believe the woman beside him is Patsy Phuzz, head of that new Belly Button Lint Guild. The fairy at the end of the row is Solomon Bundy. He looks like a nice person, but he's actually quite ruthless, which is exactly what the Itinerant Troublemakers Guild needs. I wasn't at all surprised when his guild joined. Solomon jumps at any opportunity to show what the ITG can do."

"I see members of the other guilds seated on that side of the room, but I can't tell if anyone else from the ITG is here."

"Probably not," Lionel told her. "Most of them like to keep a low profile."

"Look, there's Blue over by the judge," said Cory. "And that's Officer Deeds standing next to him."

"Is that the goblin you told me you'd *seen* in your vision?" her grandfather whispered in her ear.

Cory nodded. "He is," she whispered back. "And he's not at all nice. Oh, good, the judge is coming in now."

The courtroom grew quiet as the tall elf woman took her seat. After she asked the foreman to give the decision of the jury, everyone turned toward the box where the eleven members were seated. People seemed to hold their breath when one of the nymphs stood up holding a leaf. Cory leaned forward, eager to hear the decision.

As each verdict was announced, her heart began to soar. The jury's decision was the same for every count: the guilds were guilty.

A cheer rose from the side of the room where Cory was seated, but was quickly silenced when the judge rapped her gavel. "Court is dismissed," the elf woman declared. "I will deliver the sentences this afternoon."

"This isn't right!" shouted a voice from the other side of the room. "The guilds didn't do anything wrong!"

The few brownies who were there huddled lower in their seats while the fairies jumped to their feet, Delphinium among them. "We want a retrial!" Cory's mother shouted.

In an instant, the court was in an uproar. People shouted and frost shot through the air, freezing the judge's bench and half the empty witness stand. Three witches stood up, waving their arms to melt the frost and bind the arms of the offending fairies to their sides. The brownies tried to slink from the room while fairies rushed the judge's bench. Cory gasped when she saw her mother fling herself at the judge, who was almost out the door. Then Officer Deeds was there, grappling with Delphinium and pulling her away from the judge.

"Now is as good a time as any," her grandfather told Cory with a grin.

Cory laughed out loud. If she was going to do it, now was definitely the time. *Bow!* she thought, making time stand still. When she pulled the arrow from the quiver, it read "Delphinium Marigold Feathering." Setting the arrow to her bow, Cory shot her mother without hesitation, even though Delphinium was facing the other way. After worrying about the decision for so long, Cory suddenly knew that it was the right thing to do.

Although the arrow hit her mother in the back, it worked just as it always did. Gold sparkles were already covering Delphinium when Cory reached for the other arrow. "Wilburton Greenbough Deeds" stood out in gold letters. The moment the arrow hit the goblin officer, gold sparkles shimmered around the pair. Cory wished her bow away and sat down. Time began to move again.

No longer interested in anything but the goblin who had his arms wrapped around her waist, Delphinium let go of the judge and turned to face Officer Deeds. Cory wished she could see their expressions as their struggle became an embrace. Without Delphinium to hold her back, the judge ran from the room and slammed the door.

Although most people didn't notice what had happened between the tooth fairy and the goblin officer, at least two people did. Lionel was holding his stomach and laughing when Cory glanced his way. When she looked around the room, Laudine was laughing so hard that her shoulders were shaking. Turning her head, her eyes met Cory's. The head of WU and the most powerful witch around wiped the tears streaming down her cheeks as she nodded at her. Apparently, Lionel wasn't the only other person who thought that Cory had done the right thing.

Lionel had told the putti that there would be three people for supper that night, and he wanted it to be a special one. Cory, Blue, and Lionel ate in the family dining room, which wasn't nearly as big as the formal dining room just down the hall. It was lovely, however, with a crystal chandelier made in the shape of a bouquet of violets, Cory's grandmother's favorite flower. The color of the violets had been picked up in the vases on the mantel, some of the flowers in the chairs' upholstery, and the narrow stripes in the silk curtains. Although Cory liked all the rooms in the house, the small dining room was one of her favorites.

Lionel waited until the putti had served smoked salmon to Cory and brought perfectly grilled steaks to Blue and himself. When Orville and the two putti helping him finally left the room, Lionel turned to Cory.

"The judge pronounced the guilds' sentences about an hour ago. To be succinct, the guilds are being fined a great deal of money, their control over their members is going to be strictly curtailed, and the heads of the offending guilds are to go to jail for harassing witnesses. They can no longer punish members for quitting, nor harass them in any way."

"Thank goodness!" said Cory. "I couldn't be happier."

"We'll see about that," said Lionel. "Because I have another announcement to make. I have decided that it is time I officially retire. From now on, I will no longer perform matches, deal with the day-to-day work of a Cupid, or in any way perform a Cupid's duties. I will be here, however, should you need any advice or instruction. You are no longer a Cupid; you are now *the* Cupid in charge of matches in the land of the fey. Be forewarned, I have not been the best example for you. For a number of years now, I've not been able to travel as I once did, nor actively seek out matches. As the Cupid, you will be required to travel, sometimes great distances. Your personal life will be secondary to your duties and responsibilities as Cupid. It's just a formality at this point, but I must ask this. Corialis Feathering, will you take on this title and task of your own volition and desire?"

Cory knew that she didn't have much choice. If she didn't take on the job, no one else could do it, which meant that it wouldn't get done. Turning her back on it wouldn't stop the visions. They would just keep coming if she couldn't make the matches. She didn't really need to think about it. Besides, being Cupid had to be the most exciting and fulfilling thing she could do with her life. Wasn't that exactly what she'd wanted when she gave up being a tooth fairy? What better way to help people than to match them with their soul mates?

Before Cory could answer her grandfather, she had another promise to keep. Turning to Blue, she said, "What do you think, Blue? It's a big decision that will influence the rest of our lives."

"If it's what you want, Cory, I think you should go for it," he replied. "It's what you were born to do, isn't it?"

Cory nodded and turned back to Lionel. "I, Corialis Feathering, accept the title and responsibilities of Cupid by my own volition and desire," she said in the voice that wasn't quite her own.

"Excellent!" Lionel said as if a great weight was no longer on his shoulders. "I was waiting to do that until the court case was settled and I knew that you would be all right. Oh, before I forget to mention it, there are a number of benefits that come with the job. The house is now yours. The putti are now your employees. They will defend and assist you to the best of their abilities, and you'd be surprised what the little ones can do! Money will never be an issue for you again. There is no way to charge people for what you do, but you won't need to because you now have accounts that are always replenished. Did I forget anything? Ah, yes. You're your own boss and the only thing driving you will be your visions. Your free time is your own and you may do with it as you will. That means you don't have to give up being in your band as long as your bandmates understand that there might be times when you are unavailable. Any questions?"

Cory nodded. "You're not moving away, are you? This house is much too big for me, and I know I'm going to have lots of questions for you once I really get started."

"Don't worry, I'm not moving out yet," said her grandfather. "I'll be here until the day you get married and your husband moves in." He turned and gave Blue a pointed look. Blue smiled and nodded as if they'd reached a silent agreement.

"Since you're not nearly old enough to get married, there's plenty of time to learn your trade," Lionel continued as he turned back to Cory.

"Are you sure that you're all right with this, Blue?" Cory asked him.

Blue reached for her hand across the table. "I don't care where we live or what job you do . . . You are mine forever, which is all that really matters to me."

Don't miss the final book in the Fairy-Tale Matchmaker series!

It's wedding time for one of Cory's favorite matches!
But with another, more unexpected marriage also on
the horizon, Cory's got her hands full . . .
Will true love conquer all?

E. D. BAKER

Author of *The Frog Princess*

The Fairy→Tale

MATCHMAKER

THE MAGICAL MATCH

BLOOMSBURY

Read on for a selection from E. D. BAKER's newest book.

*C*ory shoved the letter through the mail slot in the door, rapped the door knocker three times, and ran to hide in the shrubs. Greener Pastures, the retirement community, was old-fashioned, although the residents called it quaint. No one there had message baskets the way they did in the big cities like New Town. Instead they relied on a letter carrier to go from house to house. There was only one letter carrier in Greener Pastures, so sometimes it took days or even weeks for a letter to reach its destination. Cory didn't have that kind of time. Besides, she was deliberately putting the letter in the slot at the wrong house, something a letter carrier would never do on purpose.

Cory sat down to watch the tree-stump house. Although it was only as big as her uncle Micah's garden shed, it was just the right size for a retired gnome living alone. If all went well, that situation was about to change.

Cory was the Cupid for the land of the fey. It was up to her to bring people together with their true loves. Her visions told her who belonged together. They were always right, but they didn't always come at convenient times.

Cory had taken over the job of Cupid from her grandfather only a few days before. The visions started coming thick and fast after that. Since that day, she had matched five sets of fairies, a pair of dwarves, and a human couple, all of whom lived in New Town. She'd had the vision of the two elderly gnomes for three days, but had been putting off the trip so she could handle the matches closer to home. When the visions started taking over her dreams, she knew it was the gnomes' turn.

The door opened and a man no taller than Cory's knee stepped out and looked around. He was holding Cory's envelope and he looked annoyed. "Gilbert Beanworthy, you're the worst letter carrier ever!" he shouted, although there was no one but Cory to hear him. "You know my name isn't Mildred Treesap! This isn't even my address!"

The old gnome shut the door behind him and stomped down the path to the road to look both ways. When he didn't see anyone, he grunted and started walking.

"Darn centaurs!" he grumbled. "Don't know why they'd let one be a letter carrier anyway."

Cory crept through the underbrush, following the gnome at a distance. She moved as quietly as she could, although she doubted he could hear her over his own voice. When they reached an intersection, she darted across. He still didn't see her. It took almost ten minutes to reach the address on the envelope. The old gnome complained the entire way. He didn't stop even as he left the road and turned toward a house shaped like a giant mushroom. Cory thought the bright red mushroom with big white polka dots was pretty, but the old gnome started complaining about that, too.

"Must be rich, living in a mansion like this," he muttered. "Way too fancy if you ask me."

Cory was hiding behind the tall patch of decorative grass only a few yards from the door when the gnome started knocking. Less than a minute later, a white-haired lady gnome with a sweet face opened it. "Hello?" she said when she saw the grumpy-looking gnome.

"A letter for you was misdelivered to my house," he told her.

Cory was relieved to see both people from her vision standing face-to-face. Locating the two people who she was supposed to match, then getting them in the same place at the same time wasn't always easy. Her grandfather had suggested the wrong-address method, claiming it had often worked for him.

Bow! thought Cory, and her silver bow appeared in one hand, the quiver holding two arrows in the other. Time froze for everyone but Cory as she took out the first arrow. "Timothy Alfalfa Greengrass" was written on the shaft. She set the arrow even as she walked around for a better shot, then aimed it at the male gnome's heart. It hit with a soft *plunk* amid a shower of gold sparkles.

Turning toward the lady gnome, Cory took the other arrow from the quiver. "Mildred Springleaf Treesap" read the name. This time when the arrow hit its mark, the gold sparkles engulfed both gnomes. Cory was walking away when the sparkles faded and the two fell into each other's arms. She didn't glance back until she reached the road. When she saw their tender embrace, she smiled at a job well done.

Cory landed in the backyard of the house she now shared with her grandfather. With the powerful wings of a Cupid, she could fly higher and farther than she ever could as a fairy. As long as she could take off and land out of sight, she could fly on even the sunniest of days. Keeping secret the fact that she was Cupid was always on her mind. Everyone in her household knew, of course.

Even Macks, the ogre who had become her permanent bodyguard, knew that she was Cupid. Once she'd decided to employ him like the putti who had served her grand-father for years, she had told Macks the truth. To her surprise, he had been delighted and seemed to take great pride in working for her.

"Hey, Cory!" Macks called as she walked across the yard. "How'd it go?"

Shimmer, the copper-colored baby dragon, had been flying circles around Macks. Seeing Cory, she flew straight to her, landing in her arms. Cory laughed and petted the little dragon's head, saying, "It went very well. Did anything unusual happen here?"

Macks scratched his jaw and looked thoughtful. "I don't know if I'd call it unusual, seeing that we've had so many unwanted visitors, but Shimmer and I had to chase off two more flower fairies trying to plant poison ivy in the garden."

Although the courts had ruled against the guilds that had been persecuting Cory, angry guild members were still trying to make her life miserable. It was one of the reasons Cory had decided to make Macks's job permanent. The other reason was that everyone in the household liked him and didn't want to see him go. Even the putti had asked her if he could stay.

"Thank you, Macks," said Cory. "They can't get away with much of anything with you and Shimmer patrolling the grounds. Excuse me, you two. Sarilee is already looking for me. I don't know how she knows I'm back already."

The little putti woman was standing on the back terrace with a sheaf of leaves in her hand, waiting for Cory. Without being asked, she had started acting as Cory's assistant the morning after the position of Cupid had passed from grandfather to granddaughter. Cory sometimes thought the putti woman was a little too efficient.

"I need your reports before you do anything else," Sarilee told her. "You have to do the one for this morning and two for the matches you did last night. You really should fill them out while the names are still fresh in your mind. How did the match go today?"

"Very well," Cory said as she reached down to take the leaves from the putti. "The trick with the wrong address worked perfectly."

Sarilee nodded. "That was always one of your grandfather's favorites. We received a reply from your uncle, Micah. He and Quince will be happy to join you for supper tonight."

"Thanks," Cory said as she started into the house. "I'll be in my office if anything comes up."

She passed three more putti on the way to the room she'd claimed as her office. They all grinned and waved as she walked by. Cory had agreed to keep her grandfather's helpers and was already growing fond of them. Although she'd been surprised when she first met them, she'd become so used to tiny people who looked like chubby, bald-headed babies that she no longer thought they were unusual.

Cory was seated at her desk and had just begun to fill out the leaf work when Orville knocked on the open door. The head butler and one of Cory's favorite putti, he was in charge of making sure that the household ran smoothly. When Cory waved him in, he toddled to her desk carrying a tray and saying, "Lunch won't be for another two hours, so I brought you a sandwich."

Cory grinned as he set a plate and a glass of juice in front of her. Flying long distances didn't tire her out, but it always left her with a raging appetite. She was about to take her first bite when Orville handed her a leaf. "I also brought the menu for tonight if you'd care to read it," he said.

Cory reached for the leaf. She had enjoyed taking care of her uncle's house while she lived with him. Cooking and cleaning had been ways to thank him for letting her stay there. They also kept her busy when she wasn't making matches, or doing odd jobs for people or drumming with her band, Zephyr. Moving into the big house and becoming Cupid had changed a lot of things in Cory's life. Now the putti handled all the cleaning, and the excellent chef, Creampuff, did all the cooking. Cory no longer did odd jobs for anyone, and the only matches she made were because of her visions, not because people had hired her to do them. She was still playing with Zephyr, however. It was something she swore she'd never give up. When she had the time, she'd also started to write songs on her own.

Orville waited while Cory glanced at the menu. Although she had enjoyed cooking, she knew that the putti chef's food was a hundred times better. After reading the menu, she was already looking forward to supper.

"It looks perfect," she told Orville. She was smiling at him when a vision of two very ugly ogres with oddly shaped heads and large, hairy warts came to her. She knew that other ogres would consider them very attractive, but Cory thought they were almost frightening.

"Will you be leaving soon?" asked Orville. All the putti knew that when Cory got a certain look in her eyes, she was having another vision.

Cory nodded. "But not until I've eaten this," she said, and took a bite of her sandwich.

➶➤

Cory was off making more matches until late afternoon. When she came back, she tried to hurry through the leaf work before her uncle, Micah, and his fiancée, Quince, arrived. She was looking forward to seeing Micah again and getting to know Quince.

Setting the leaves in the basket for Sarilee to collect, Cory hurried to her room to change her clothes. She loved the bedroom and adjoining bathing room that she'd chosen, as well as the fact that she didn't have to share either one with anyone other than Shimmer. After brushing her hair and changing into a new green dress made of silk, she hurried to the stairs.

Cory was partway down the elegant staircase when the door opened and Blue walked in. Johnny Blue was half ogre, half human. He was over seven feet tall, which was short for an ogre, and tall for a human. He also had a rough, craggy face, which many people found unattractive, but he was handsome in Cory's eyes. He was an officer-in-training at the Fey Law Enforcement Agency, or FLEA, as most people called it. More importantly, he was Cory's very own true love. Like Macks, he had a room on the first floor of the big house and was there when Cory needed him. Protecting the love of his life was his top priority.

Blue looked up and saw Cory. Opening his arms, he waited as she ran down the last few steps and into his embrace. They kissed, and Cory knew that whatever else might happen, everything was all right as long as he was there.

"Ahem!" Orville was standing by the door to the hallway. "Beverages are being served on the back terrace," he announced before walking away.

"I got called into the chief's office today," Blue said as he and Cory walked hand in hand toward the terrace. "It seems that I've put in enough hours and my work has been good enough that I don't have to wait the full year to take the Culprit Interrogator test."

"That's wonderful!" Cory cried. "Congratulations!"

"I'm afraid it means that I'll have to spend most of my free time studying. The test is next month."

"Then I'll tell everyone to be extra quiet around you so you can concentrate," Cory told him.

"Why do we need to be quiet around Blue?" her grandfather asked as he joined them in the hallway.

"He's going to be studying for his CI test!" Cory replied. "Isn't that wonderful!"

"It is indeed," said Lionel. "But I must say that I'm not surprised. I've heard only good things about your work, young man. Imagine, a CI in the family!"

Although Cory and Blue were waiting until they were older, everyone knew that they were going to get married someday. The only family member who hadn't given them her blessing was Cory's mother, Delphinium, who didn't seem to approve of anything Cory had done once she'd quit the Tooth Fairy Guild.

Cory, Blue, and Lionel had just accepted glasses of berry juice from the putti carrying a tray when Micah and Quince walked through the glass doors onto the terrace. Cory hadn't seen her uncle since the day she moved out of his house. Setting her glass on a table, she hurried to give him a welcoming hug. "It's so good to see you!" she told him.

"You too!" he replied. "How is everything?"

"Busy," Cory said, and turned to Quince. It felt natural to give her a hug, too.

"I've been looking forward to meeting you!" said Quince. "A few minutes in my office doesn't count," she added with a laugh. "How is your woodchuck doing, by the way?"

Quince, a chiropractor for animals, had treated Weegie, the woodchuck, for a sore back. Cory had *seen* Quince in a vision, and knew that she'd finally found the match for Micah.

"She's fine," Cory said. "Actually, we have two woodchucks living with us. Weegie and Noodles have dug a den in the woods down by the river."

"Go long!" Macks shouted to Shimmer as they came around the house. The ogre threw a ball and the baby dragon shot after it, catching the ball with her front talons.

Quince gasped when she turned and saw them. "Micah said you had a baby dragon! She's adorable!"

"And very talented," said Lionel.

Micah was introducing his fiancée to Cory's grandfather when Orville toddled out of the house. "If you would all care to come inside, dinner will be served shortly," he announced.

"Good, because I'm famished," Cory said. Taking Blue's hand, she started for the door.

"Any idea what we're having tonight?" Blue asked her.

"Stir-fried vegetables," said Cory. "And roast beef for people who like meat."

Ogres loved meat and Blue was half ogre. He'd been doing without it lately because Cory had been raised as a fairy and was still a vegetarian. She appreciated Creampuff's efforts to make everyone happy.

"Roast beef, huh?" Blue said, and smacked his lips. "That chef sure knows the way to a man's heart!"

Cory laughed. "Should I be jealous?"

"Never," Blue said as he picked her up and spun her around. "I'd take you over roast beef any day!"

Because there were only five of them, they ate in the family dining room. Cory was enjoying her vegetables when Quince turned to her and said, "I have a favor to ask of you. Would you be my maid of honor? It would mean a lot to Micah and to me if you were part of our wedding."

"I'd be delighted!" Cory cried. "And if there's anything I can do to help, just let me know."

"I was hoping you'd say that," said Quince. "The wedding is only a week and a half away. I thought I could handle it all, but I'm getting a little overwhelmed."

"Actually, I might be able to help," said Lionel. "I was wondering if you two would like to hold your wedding here. You can have it inside if it rains or on the back lawn if it's sunny. Either way, you can invite as many people as you'd like. Creampuff would be happy to prepare all the food."

"That's a very kind offer," Micah told him, "but Quince and I have already decided that we want to have a simple wedding in the park across the street from my house."

"I'd be happy to help you with whatever you need," Cory told Quince. "Let me know what you want me to do and—"

A high, thin shriek made everyone look around. It seemed to be coming from the fireplace. When the sound faded, Lionel gestured to Orville and said, "Please go find out what made that awful racket."

"Of course, sir," said Orville. He was back a few minutes later. "It appears that Shimmer lit her fire under some fairies who were attempting to drop weasels down the chimneys."

"How odd," said Lionel. "I wonder why they chose weasels."

"I think I can answer that," said Blue. "When I finally caught up with the fairies who had brought rats to the Shady Nook when Zephyr was performing, one of them told me that they had paid a deposit on the rats, hoping to collect them and take them back to the rental shop the next day. The fairy was irate that the shape-shifter in the audience had turned into a cat and eaten them all. I can only assume that the shop was out of rats and the fairies who came by just now thought that weasels were the closest thing."

"Do you think they paid a deposit on the weasels, too?" asked Cory. "What kind of a shop rents such things anyway?"

"A vermin rental shop, I suppose," said Lionel.

"Are the fairies still coming after you?" Micah asked Cory. "I thought they would stop after the guilds lost the trial."

"I think losing just made them madder," said Cory. "Macks patrols the grounds with Shimmer off and on all day. Ever since the trial he's chased away a couple of dozen fairies who were trying to do something nasty. The poor putti who takes care of the garden is forever pulling up poison ivy and thistles that the flower fairies keep planting."

"The flower fairies have been especially mad ever since Flora Petalsby, the head of their guild, was sent to jail," said Blue.

"What about the Tooth Fairy Guild?" asked Micah. "Have you heard anything from Delphinium?"

Cory shook her head. "Mother doesn't want to talk to me any more than I want to talk to her now. If I'm lucky, it will stay that way for a very long time. I doubt that I'll be invited to her wedding, whatever kind she chooses."

E. D. BAKER is the author of the Tales of the Frog Princess series, the Wide-Awake Princess series, the Fairy-Tale Matchmaker series, the Magic Animal Rescue series, and many other delightful books for young readers, including *Fairy Wings*, *Fairy Lies*, and *A Question of Magic*. Her first book, *The Frog Princess*, was the inspiration for Disney's hit movie *The Princess and the Frog*. She lives with her family and their many animals in Maryland.

www.talesofedbaker.com

Enter the magical world of
E. D. Baker!

www.talesofedbaker.com